Imagination Reimagined
Not Your Children's Fairy Tales

Edited by
L. Andrew Cooper,
Georgia L. Jones,
and Christopher Kokoski

a BlackWyrm book
Louisville, Kentucky

IMAGINATION REIMAGINED:
  NOT YOUR CHILDREN'S FAIRY TALES

A BlackWyrm Book
BlackWyrm Publishing
10307 Chimney Ridge Ct, Louisville, KY 40299

Printed in the United States of America.

ISBN: 978-1-61318-163-8

Cover Design by Dave Mattingly
Edited by L. Andrew Cooper, Georgia L. Jones, Christopher Kokoski

First edition: April 2014

A Note from the Editors

The sweet fairy tales kids know today have little connection with the awful stories about people or animals making bad decisions and facing gruesome results that flourished in Northern European oral traditions and, after they were collected by the likes of Charles Perrault and the Brothers Grimm from the 1600s through the 1800s, got the "fairy" title. *Imagination Reimagined* reminds you first that fairy tales aren't necessarily kids' stuff, and second that such tales *live* because we retell them to help us see who we are now. I dedicate my contributions to the students working with me at the University of Louisville.

L. Andrew Cooper

Imagination Reimagined was a special project for me. Not only was it my debut editing project, but fairy tales have always held a special place in my heart. As a child, these were my first introduction to fantastic worlds that were full of adventure... and I liked it. Fairy tales set the perfect stage for a lifetime of moral and safety concerns. At a very young age, I learned to always look for ears on grandma, that eavesdropping on your parents may save your life, and to leave the house building to the bricklayers. May your fairy tales always have happy endings!

Georgia L. Jones

Escape, emotion, entertainment – you'll experience all, dear reader, within the stories in this book. A brief mental getaway. A welcome reprieve from reality with all its seeming coincidence and humdrum happenings. You, dear reader, won't find anything humdrum in this collection of stories.

Fairy tales might be the best of stories, having survived the test of time, of telling and retelling. The stories within this book reshape classic children's tales, sometimes in humorous ways, sometimes in horrific. I dare you to try and read just one...

Christopher Kokoski

Contents

Kindertotenlieder

(songs for dead children, as played by a pied piper in New Hamelin, Kentucky)
by L. Andrew Cooper

When the silhouette appeared in Maryanne's bedroom doorway, its shoulders created a broad triangle that tapered to almost nothing at the waist before flaring into rough-jeaned rods of legs that stemmed from a midsection wrapped so tightly that even in the dark, even from the distance of her bed, it seemed to throb. Leaping shadows provided contour and definition that would otherwise be lacking in the hairless chest as it approached her candlelit nest between pillows and satin sheets, next to the nightstand where the clock read midnight exactly.

Carrie's boy, from two doors down.

The boy who delivered newspapers from his bicycle, the kid Maryanne took to Boy Scout meetings when his mom had to work late at the job she'd taken to keep the family fed since the war started. Maryanne had known him all his life, but she had never seen this look, or smelled this smell, the way he entered her at the eyes and nose at the same time, handsome musk intoxicating, and she must have been out of her mind to feel her hips begin to writhe against the sheets, to imagine and to beckon for the weight of him on top of her, inside of her.

His name was Scott. He was sixteen. Maryanne was forty-nine. She hadn't had sex with anyone since cancer had taken her husband five years ago. She'd never been with a man younger than thirty, even when she'd lost her own virginity as a teen. Younger men, boys, didn't appeal to her. But Scott took a step, and another, and she was watching herself as she launched from the covers, ripped at the button on his jeans, and pulled him to her for the rest.

Under a thin sliver of waning moon, twenty-two women in New Hamelin got pregnant that night. The next night, and the night after, when the sky looked like God had inked out the stars and moon, more than fifty others joined their number. By the end of that lunar cycle, almost every fertile woman in New Hamelin was pregnant. By March of 1944, New Hamelin was having an unprecedented baby boom – more than a year before the majority of able-bodied men aged eighteen to thirty-eight returned home after the victories in Europe and the Pacific.

The morning after her encounter with her sixteen-year-old neighbor, Maryanne sat in the bathtub, shower running hot, turning pink skin to red. She didn't know why she had done it. She couldn't understand. She'd never understand.

***

New Hamelin was dying.

The Japs dropping bombs in Hawaii, a tragedy of course, was almost a godsend because it gave so many unemployed men new purpose. They'd been doubly disheartened to have gotten back to work only to be put out again because of a cave-in that took half the coal mine that paid the town's bills. Now they had an enemy more tangible than the longing in their families' faces. The people they left felt the necessary happiness of patriotism, at first, but gradually they began to realize that making a home for the boys to return to was their responsibility, and they didn't have much of a clue how to do it.

Then, out of nowhere, came what one preacher called "an epidemic of fornication," a sin that was its own punishment, for it brought lives with mouths that needed feeding. By the time the epidemic had run its course, the town had more than one hundred new babies, more than one hundred new voices wailing for food, crammed under roofs barely large enough to shelter the families already beneath them, so nobody slept, day and night, ceaseless wailing, and they planted gardens, and they went through town reserves, and they begged from nearby towns, and they asked for government assistance, but didn't they know there was a war on?

People needed to be doing their parts, not asking for handouts. Not at a time like this.

A time like this. A desperate time. And desperate times....

Maryanne didn't even think she should have been able to have a baby. Not at her age. Some kid shouldn't have been able to slink into her room, late at night, and leave behind this screaming infant, begging for food, her breasts raw, insufficient. It shouldn't have been, and yet it was, and she was angry. Didn't she have a right to be angry?

Not far from her house a mountain jutted up with one smooth, sloping edge and another sharp and angular, from top to bottom a deep plunge into bone-piercing jags of rock. Anger, and desperation. She climbed the mountain that day not planning on coming back down, at least not breathing. Other women worried about how they would explain their mewling surprises when their men got home. Maryanne had no such worry. She would be alone, with this unwanted screaming, forever.

At the top, overlooking the place where she imagined shearing forces of stone rending her like tissue paper, a stranger waited. In her fingers, pressed against her lips, the stranger held a simple recorder, the kind children trained on before choosing which woodwind or brass instrument they really wanted to play. It wasn't some plastic or cheap bamboo, though, and its sounds were neither harsh nor hollow. The fine wood, streaked and mottled in a pattern that might have been natural and might have been some exquisite design that mimicked nature, translated the air from the woman's lips into sounds of sweet airy lightness, pitches of absolute precision, breath-stealing harmonies, and lilting progressions of such melancholy, punctuated with pulse-fluttering trills, that Maryanne thought she had never quite heard music as beautiful.

"Come then, Maryanne, and tell me how much you know," the strange woman with the recorder said. The greyish-white streaks in her hair were so regular that the long waves running along her neck and shoulders looked like bleeding stripes of auburn and silver, and the lines around her eyes, which seemed to project shadows instead of capturing light, changed with every slight turn of her head, making her age impossible to discern.

A moment after the striped woman's question settled between them, she played a few more notes on the recorder and spoke again. "My name is Matilda Roan," she said. "And I know why you're here."

"Matilda," Maryanne repeated. Roan. Like a horse. Glancing again at the colors in the woman's hair, Maryanne almost laughed. "Why am I here?"

The strange woman lifted the recorder to her lips and played a series of notes that sounded familiar, a melody Maryanne couldn't quite pick out, something that resonated with church or childhood that she could not name.

Beneath them, where the tree line gave way to naked crags of stone, flocks of birds burst from branches and leaves, filling the sky like a bucket of pebbles tossed into the ocean. Above them, bramble and moss still clung to the rocks, and with a look from Matilda, they ignited, forming a curved shell of flame above the birds, which rose in the air like sediment sunk in water. With the same volition as the pebbles their rising formation resembled, the birds drifted into the fire and became, one by one, flapping, squawking, panicked, winged bright balls of light before they snuffed and fell like ash, raining to the earth below just as Maryanne had imagined throwing her own body to die on the rocks just minutes before Matilda had introduced herself.

"I can help," Matilda said.

She shouldn't have understood, but somehow, Maryanne did. "How?"

Matilda gazed out toward the river, barely visible beneath the horizon. Maryanne wondered how many of the soldiers would return by ship. She imagined a vast homecoming to a bevy of wives weighted by babies whose fathers were not the veteran husbands, and she imagined the reactions to all the little cuckoos, and she tried to think of an explanation – a rash of alien, sexless impregnations? some sort of government test? – and realized that variations on her own truth, the sweaty night she had spent with a boy barely old enough to be fertile, was the most likely and believable explanation for any of them. This unwanted generation would force every truth into a light that would burn them all as surely as those birds had turned to ash and rained quietly back into the trees.

"In three days," Matilda said, "I will come to the town hall at sunset. If you and the mayor would rather avoid the consequences of this town's... indiscretions... I can help, as long as you offer me something worthwhile in return. If you are not there, you will never see me again."

Maryanne was nobody, certainly not someone to keep company with Mayor Trimble, but New Hamelin was small enough for her to request and get a meeting with him the same day, as long as she understood that he would (pretend to) be very busy and only (act like he would) have very limited time to listen to her concerns.

Mayor Trimble, in the midst of refusing to join Maryanne to await New Hamelin's strange visitor in three days' time, stopped when he saw all eyes in his office – his receptionist, his press secretary, the woman who had taken over accounting since her husband had shipped out – all of them with newborns at home – glaring.

Three sunsets later, he and Maryanne stood on the town hall's front steps and watched the Roan woman approach, the horizon behind her, her outline a blaze while her face was a shadow distinguished only by the cylinder she held to her lips. Soft, lulling notes turned each head as she passed. Trimble placed a hand on his unsteady chest.

Maryanne held her baby. She had nowhere else to leave it. Until Matilda had appeared on the walkway leading to the town hall, the boy had screamed almost incessantly, but the first note from the recorder turned his screams to coos. She looked at his round face, the spittle dotting his pouty lips, the giant blue eyes, and she once again considered whether she should have just written her own father's name on the birth certificate instead of making up a story about filling in the name after a baptism she never intended to have. She didn't understand why—

Matilda Roan shook her head. No. Maryanne understood full well why she had refused to name the boy. Many of her neighbors had done the same. Perhaps all of them.

Maryanne felt a dawning realization, and nausea arose with tears inside of her, both threatening to spill, when Matilda said, "Enough."

"Pardon me, ma'am?" Mayor Trimble asked.

"Enough waiting." Matilda played a note and let it hang in the air, becoming a blanket over the town. Maryanne felt it like a tingle inside of her, in her chest, between her legs, in her head. "We all know what you need, but tell me anyway."

The mayor looked to his left and right. The three of them, he and Maryanne and the strange visitor, were far enough from the small crowd for their voices to be unheard. "We need," Mayor Trimble said, and he cleared his throat, "not to have... had this... recent... population... increase."

Matilda laughed. "Then you don't need me. You need a time machine, and maybe much more." The recorder pressed against her lips, a succession of notes began, and she turned to walk away.

"Wait!" the mayor called.

Maryanne watched the exchange, as terrified that Matilda would return as she was that the strange woman would leave.

Matilda returned, and the mayor said, "I'm not asking you to change the past." He faked a laugh, and the contrast with Matilda's more genuine mirth caused a twisting pain in Maryanne's chest. "But what can you do about the present?" Mayor Trimble was almost whispering.

"If your people have the will, I can take what they have and make it easier for them. I can make all of this into a bad dream from which they can awake tomorrow with fewer mouths to feed."

Maryanne looked down at the baby in her arms, and then her eyes met the mayor's. Nearby, in the small but growing crowd on the town hall's lawn, mothers repeated Maryanne's gesture, looking first at their offspring and then to their leader to pull the trigger that they could not.

"All right then," the man said. Maryanne saw that his eyes were closed. "Do it."

"Not so easy," Matilda said. A rapid rendition of the first phrase from "Yankee Doodle" rang out from her recorder. "The last ten years taught too many girls like me that we can't live on charity alone. What are you offering?"

The mayor wiped a sweaty palm along the side of his expensive jacket. "We don't have much," he said. "What do you want?"

"Something you won't miss," Matilda answered. "Keep the good part, but sign the collapsed section of the mine over to me."

This time the mayor's laugh sounded more genuine. "I'm afraid that doesn't belong to the town, so it's not ours to give. It belongs to a company—"

"That you own," Matilda finished. "We have witnesses. A handshake will suffice. Promise the collapsed portion of the mine to me, and the quiet you hear right now," and she gestured to the lawn with mother-arms filled by quiet squirming newborns, "will remain."

The mayor, about to object, found the crowd on the lawn much larger than it had been mere minutes ago. Dozens of mothers with peaceful children in their arms awaited his response. "It's yours," the mayor said.

He shook Matilda's hand, and Maryanne saw something in his face the moment they touched. Worse than a grimace: the look on the mayor's face was the same as a child hearing Santa, or maybe an adult hearing God, was just a fairy tale told to create an illusion of balance in a world where people in the land of New Hamelin's ancestors were supposedly using special camps for mass murder. That handshake took the whole town someplace new, a place where Europe and all the rest of it might make sense.

***

The tones rising from Matilda's recorder sounded unlike anything Maryanne had yet heard from the instrument, at once sweet and insistent, soft and commanding, gentle and irresistible, latching itself like a hook in the center of her chest and pulling her by a thread as the strange woman began a march.

The other women gathered on the town hall's lawn, babes in arms, followed similar invisible tethers. Matilda led them in a cluster attached by silk threads to her fingers, which made a melody on the recorder with enough harmonic resonance to simulate an orchestra. First one and then two and then a flock of baby-carrying women followed her down Main Street, slowly converging on the point where road met river. As the women soared behind their musical, mystical leader, bobbing on their feet in smiling delirium, more emerged from houses and side streets, swelling the ranks of Matilda's followers until the invisible tethers were so many that they became tangled, and the women's paths became confused, wrapping around one another, bumping and correcting their courses, never losing their leader but not quite keeping themselves. They swarmed like inane gnats, but still the music kept them flying and kept them moving toward the water.

When they reached the river, Matilda did not hesitate. She waded in, playing notes that got sweeter and more familiar, no longer following intervals from the do-re-mi scale Maryanne had learned in choir, but a different scale entirely, more chromatic, more dissonant, but with its own beauty, its own compulsion, even as Matilda stepped so deep into the water that it lapped against her chin.

Matilda's knot of infant-toting gnats dragged behind her, cutting through water as if it offered no more resistance than air. As their legs, middles, torsos, arms, and necks submerged, they didn't notice what was in their arms.

Maryanne heard noises, almost unrecognizable, the infants screaming until the water choked off the sounds. Taking a deep breath, she realized only Matilda needed to stay where she was, to keep playing the recorder. Maryanne dove into the water, loving its cold on her face, feeling her hair begin to run with the currents, not noticing the bundle that slipped away from her, slowly sinking and drifting away.

***

The next morning, Maryanne awoke late. She found herself in her own bed, not remembering how she had gotten there, but she felt refreshed, as if a tight collar around her neck had been loosened, and finally, she could breathe. Sun poured through her windows. Slipping on a simple dress, she walked out into the bright morning. Women all along her street seemed to be doing the same thing, stretching as they emerged from their front doors, arms reaching up as if in greeting to the sun.

Quiet.

Two doors down, Carrie greeted the morning, and her son Scott followed her into the yard. His face lacked the wonder-of-the-day elation that seemed to engulf the women in their stretches. He stared directly at Maryanne, and the stare was like an itch in Maryanne's brain. Something—

Her hands running along his broad chest, thumbs touching as they came together over his navel, fingers curling around...

Oh God. This boy had gotten her pregnant. And then the baby—

In one direction from Maryanne's house, the mountain where birds had exploded into ash-rain loomed over New Hamelin. In the opposite direction, the river snaked by. Well-fed.

"Wait," she said to no one. The word meant nothing, but she had nothing else to say as she walked, jogged, ran, then sprinted toward the water. Some of her neighbors followed. They reached the spot where they'd all followed Matilda into the water and saw no trace of what they'd done. Had it been a dream?

Maryanne turned, and with steps she forced to be firm, she moved downriver, watching the shifting textures of the surface for signs of floating things. Her eyes stayed fixed on the water, so she tripped when her feet met the first clump on the shore.

Women behind her yelped.

Maryanne fell face-first into the dirt but felt objects beneath her, solid enough to poke and bruise, but soggy and soft as well. She pushed herself up. Before she looked down to see what had been pressing against her dress, she glanced forward and saw the other clumps, some small, just two or three, and some larger piles, harder to count without getting closer.

She had stumbled onto the spot where the bodies had washed ashore. The stench of incipient rot, bloated by river water and the gnawing of whatever had a taste for newborn flesh beneath the surface, unveiled itself, and Maryanne vomited. Some of the other women were doing the same. Before them, more than a hundred tiny blue corpses announced the town's crime. Matilda had solved the problem, but she had not cleaned the mess.

***

Assured by nothing more than Maryanne's instincts, Mayor Trimble again waited on the town hall's steps at sunset, and indeed, the strange Roan woman, the recorder at her side, her lips free and grinning, approached the bottom of the steps and bowed to her employer. "Have I not completed my task?"

The look on the man's face offered clear loathing. "You did not," he said. "We did not ask you to make us dig a mass grave."

"But you should, though, and if you are clever, you should leave it unmarked," Matilda said. "And then, your problem is gone. I gave you what you needed. I didn't promise to be your maid. When your town's war heroes return, they will find New Hamelin the same image of virtue they left."

Maryanne didn't notice the mayor's sidearm until he was aiming it at Matilda's head. "This entire town witnessed you commit mass murder."

Matilda laughed. "This entire town committed mass murder. No one witnessed me do anything," she said, raising the recorder to her lips, "but play."

Before she could begin a string of notes, Trimble interrupted: "Don't you dare." He pulled back the hammer on his pistol.

"I'm sure you can find a stake and plenty of kindling in the woods at the mountain's foot. Wouldn't you rather burn me alive?" The look on Matilda Roan's face was coquettish. She even fluttered her eyelashes.

Maryanne felt sure that, even from the bottom of the steps, Matilda could see Mayor Trimble's finger tightening on the trigger.

All at once, she understood why. Matilda was right: the entire town had committed mass murder, and those who hadn't killed the babies directly had illicitly fathered them, tacitly approved their deaths, or both. Matilda, somehow, was the only person in the town not guilty. And for that, Maryanne knew, Mayor Trimble's finger would not stop.

The gunshot rang out, and none of the crowd on the lawn looked away as the bullet tore through the Roan woman's breast in a spray of red. She did not fall. The hand not holding the recorder rose, its first gesture a stop. "You refuse the promised payment?"

Mayor Trimble fired again, this time landing a bullet somewhere in Matilda's ribs.

Without a word, Matilda turned her back to the mayor, whose third shot missed. She began to play, beginning this time with the dissonant, chromatic scale she had transitioned to yesterday and then moving into something worse, sounds that seemed to operate not on the ears but on the surface of the skin, and then on the muscle, and then on the bone. Matilda began to march the same path as the day before, toward the river, and again, the people on the lawn followed her. Maryanne followed her, and this time, Mayor Trimble followed her, too. Men and women gathered to her as they traversed the path to the river, but instead of mindless, gnat-like fluttering, they moved in militant formation, an army.

A twitching army.

As they moved, Maryanne saw that they were changing. First she just thought Carrie, who had worn her hair short since the 20s, had grown her hair out a bit, but then she realized the new growth surrounded her, not just on people's heads, but on their faces, their arms, every bit of exposed skin, and from the tickling, itching sensations all over her body, Maryanne guessed that they were all sprouting these coarse, grey hairs everywhere. Walking further, their posture began to change. Backs stooped, necks lowered while chins jutted upward, and elbows bent so that limp wrists hovered near whiskered cheeks. The army's gait became loping, not an easy march but a group propulsion that was increasingly unsteady.

Maryanne was the first to fall, but she caught herself with her hands. Continuing on all fours was much easier and much faster. She scurried over two of the people in front of her so she could get a closer look at Matilda, who played such beautiful, awful sounds, pitches totally alien, in registers Maryanne could never have heard before, but her ears were bigger now, capturing more, and she loved it.

A weird pain wracked her hindquarters. Alarmed, she turned to face its cause, but she realized someone had just accidentally stepped on her tail.

At last, they reached the long stretch of shore covered with newborn corpses, blue and bloated from drowning. The sharpness of Maryanne's new teeth would hardly be necessary.

Matilda turned to face her new army of rats, and she gestured toward the field of bodies. In less than an hour, only a few bones remained.

After Ever

by William I. Levy

Despite her tears, Kim kept the radio on. The announcer's voice was distracting.

And the sound from the old hand-cranked device drowned out most of the noise from the cold streets. Even if she'd dared, at its loudest the receiver was overwhelmed by an occasional heartrending scream.

The slender young woman hid in the shelter of a cold, dark apartment. Huddled in a blanket, she fed bits of cloth and shredded furniture to a tiny fire in an old Dutch oven on some hot pads. The musty smell was overwhelmed by acrid scents from outside she was afraid to identify.

Eventually Kim grew too weary for the misery and fear. Soft brown eyes dried as she dozed lightly, dreams of the past sparked by the newscasts.

***

"You seem like a reliable person." The white-haired man spoke slowly, each word graced with grave consideration. "Perhaps you could help me with a problem."

Ten-year-old Kimberly had quickly grown bored with the art show and the seemingly endless series of grimly untouchable displays. This gentle voice offering respect was at least different, interesting.

Still, you couldn't be too careful. She checked, and her parents were watching.

A tentative nod of her honey-brown head.

Worn fingers fumbled with a black silk bag. "Here, hold your hands out, cupped. Careful, now."

Sunlight sparkled as cool weight settled lightly into her palms. A small sphere, half glass, half charcoal, occupied her gaze. Kimberly could feel her parents drawn closer by curiosity.

Looking into the transparent side, the young girl noticed that the interior seemed curiously deep. In fact, she could see much further than the opaque side. As if her fingers weren't even in the way.

"What do you see?" The ancient man asked softly.

"Swirls of silver dust, and, and a cat with a penguin?" Kimberly answered hesitantly. "Is that right?"

"Everyone sees something different. But that's quite good." He smiled in approval, and she felt a flash of pride.

Drinking in the mystery of this tiny wonder, Kimberly softly asked. "What is it?"

"A hole in the universe." Came the calm answer as sure hands retrieved it, holding the sphere almost reverently. "We should be careful, here. It's more than a little dangerous."

Her parents looked over her shoulder at the cosmic marvel and chuckled at the grandiose statement.

Kimberly was startled to notice her own level of annoyance at their lack of awe flicker across the old man's face.

"It's my responsibility, taking care of it." He continued nonetheless. "I've got a few talismans, objects of power to help with the task..."

The old man fished around in the bag, removed a handful of items.

"Clarity of Starry Night." Gnarled, strong fingers offered a small purple sphere. In its not-quite-black depths, a thousand tiny silver stars twinkled. "Knowing the hidden ways."

Kimberly returned it gravely as he handed her the next one, a pale, translucent thumb-sized egg. As she held it, the edges glowed with a fierce gold.

"Dawn That Always Comes. Hope that never fails."

The final talisman was a faceted chip. As it lay in her hand, a series of faint rainbows spread along her palm.

"Deepest Rainbow." He smiled wistfully. "The most powerful, but also the most difficult to use. The gift to show others your true heart."

"Wow." Kimberly's eyes were wide as he continued.

"As I said, I need help." He sighed, glanced at the adults.

Bored with the lack of spectacle, they'd already moved on to the next booth. The old man shook his head in resigned disgust.

"Protecting the hole uses up all my time. Keeping it from growing, or moving about," he said seriously. "I need somebody reliable and clever to come up with a way to actually fix it."

"Oh. Yeah, I can try to do that." Kimberly said earnestly.

"Excellent." The old man smiled. "I had a feeling. But, stalwart and brave lass that you are, it couldn't hurt to have a bit of fey help, would it? Which talisman fits you, I wonder?"

He held out the trio in a slightly shaking palm.

Kimberly didn't hesitate. "Deepest Rainbow."

A furry gray eyebrow twitched as his smile grew larger. "I knew you were the one. Take it, and remember your promise."

Unlike real life, in the dream a suddenly grown up Kim held the glittering gem near her heart reverently. "I remember. I'll do my best to find a way to fix it."

"Good girl." The silver-bearded man chuckled softly. "Now, you'd best rejoin your elders."

"Oh, shoot!" Once more a child, Kimberly was off like a rocket, dashing along the line of booths to catch up with her distracted parents.

In the dream, as happened originally, when her father insisted on revisiting to the old man's booth to pay for or return the gem, they couldn't locate him among the confusing maze of craftspeople and displays.

***

Kim woke as the flame sputtered, panic spurring her to dump a whole handful of cloth on the feeble fire. She barely managed to restrain herself, carefully feeding it tiny scraps until orange flickers danced again in agile strength. Dim light crept through her refuge.

A few little splinters of chair leg inserted at angles, and the numb, frightened woman felt safe enough to relax.

She gave the radio a few vigorous cranks and listened wearily to the public channel.

"It's three am Eastern Standard time in the Ohio Valley. At the top of the news; No progress on determining responsibility for the disastrous attack on the CERN Labs last week." The announcer's voice was unfamiliar, reedy and unsuitable for a broadcaster. Considering the circumstances, though... "The United Nations has issued yet another call for an emergency, international open pooling of physicists, particle and others, to handle the crisis. China has joined the list of nations refusing to cooperate, claiming the so-called accidental black hole release is an American-backed European Union hoax to gain access to their weapons research programs."

"Why can't anybody convince them to see?" Kim pleaded sleepily. "We've gotta work together for once..."

The announcer offered no answer. "Meanwhile, estimates of as high as a million refugees are fleeing the new, active volcano in the south of France. Multiple chain earthquakes continue..."

Dozing off again, Kim escaped cruel reality into crueler dreams.

***

"You can't do that!" She stamped a foot. The impact of her canvas sneaker lacked dramatic emphasis.

Looming over her, Tony shrugged. "Somebody's gotta do something, and after that quake it's a sure bet the morons at City Hall can't handle things anymore. Don't see why it shouldn't be us. Those damned scientists murdered the world. They deserve to suffer."

"That, that's so..." She tried not to cry. "First off, whoever blew up the CERN caused the tiny black hole that's burrowing through the Earth, making earthquakes and volcanoes. Second, scientists are people like us, not aliens or wizards. And last, Dr. Barry's just a high school teacher!"

"Shoulda guessed you for a lousy science symp." Her boyfriend stood, made a point of checking his rifle. "Nobody's gonna listen to a poor little girl anyway. Don't worry about big things. Keep your mouth shut and I'll protect you. But you better get your pretty head straight by the time we're finished with your geek buddy." His laugh as he turned to leave had a menacing edge.

To her surprise, Kim had already decided. Tony hadn't even made it out of the apartment when she managed to clock him from behind with a small cast-iron skillet.

"I guess you're not moving in after all." The usually indecisive woman managed not to fall completely apart. Shaking, she stripped his ammo belt and set the rifle to one side, then rolled the comatose young man into the hall and nervously locked the door.

In the dream his moans seemed to last forever, as the gun leaning against the wall swelled, becoming a mammoth monument to regret and guilt.

***

This time she woke whimpering. Outside, male voices bellowed in anger, and for a moment she thought one of them was Tony.

But the cries died down before Kim could bring herself to risk opening a window.

Fortunately, the security bars hadn't been dislodged by the, what had the announcer said? '5.5 quake,' she remembered vaguely.

Most people hadn't paid attention to the disastrous destruction in France, with typical disinterest in anything outside the national border. But when the massive micro-phenomenon began an irregular spiral burning a line through the Earth's crust, it literally shattered any parochial illusions of sanctity.

Locally, power went out with the initial shocks. Fire and panic rioting stopped any organized efforts to restore services. Kim was grateful she at least somehow still had water, although she'd filled the tub just in case.

Her single foray outside post-quake with Tony had been a nightmare two-block journey to a government emergency relief center. Grim adults stood around in tiny clusters, while even the smallest children sat quietly nearby. She got the distinct impression of unfocussed trouble looking for targets, and was grateful to have Tony and his rifle to hide behind.

They'd gotten small boxes of odd tasting cheese, dried meat, raisins, powdered milk, bland crackers, and a few other random items. The workers were apologetic, but the few comments were complaints. Everyone in line looked haunted, spoke of end times and doom. She'd wanted to talk to them, try to comfort some of the older neighbors, but Tony saw no value in it, had insisted on leaving quickly for safety's sake.

That was nearly a week ago, and Kim dreaded the hopeless madness waiting outside.

She sat back, relaxing against the cool faux stone of a decorative arch. A hand instinctively rested for a moment on the gentle curve between her slight breasts. A wry smile crossed her lips at the decade old habit.

Pulling a worn leather cord, Kim drew a black silk pouch from under her blouse. Hesitating for a moment, she opened it. A long-treasured thumb-sized faceted oval dropped into her palm.

"Deepest Rainbow." The young woman sighed in comfort as tiny, red-hued arcs spawned by the fire's glow danced among her fingers.

Entranced, Kim was startled to notice the initial bloom of morning crawling through the window.

"Dawn That Always Comes. Hope's good." She murmured vaguely. "But where's Clarity of Starry Night when I need to know the hidden ways?"

The first clear beam of sunlight lanced across the sill, striking the quartz gem, blazing into a brilliant rainbow.

Kim stared at it, shook as if freed from a terrible spell.

Clutching the sparkling crystal, she stood, reborn determination filling her eyes with an equally intense fire.

From deep inside and long ago, ten-year-old Kimberly spoke up fiercely. "Somebody has to fix the hole."

Kim opened the door to her apartment and strode forth into chaos, armed only with rainbows.

Thence?

Not By the Hair of My Chinny Chin Chin

by Christopher Kokoski

Dead bodies lay everywhere.

Gut turning to ice, Channing digested the carnage. Even dismembered and cast across the wooden floor of his parents' cabana, they were easy to identify. The remains of his family.

The spacious chamber had devolved into chaos, decorated in crimson splotches and mutilated skeletal scaffolding, the meat nearly stripped from the bone.

He couldn't breathe.

They're all dead. His gaze fell on a smaller, child-sized frame topped by a skull that grinned up at him from below two empty eye sockets. Isabelle. My niece. Where pigtails usually bounced, now only a smooth bowl of bone remained.

Knees buckling, he sank to the wood-paneled floor, a weak moan on his lips. The room pivoted as if on a turntable.

Only when the room settled again did the smell register its full intensity, a rotting stench that grasped at his lungs and called to mind heaping human remains from his recent 16-month stint in the desert. He clutched his stomach and vomited on the floor.

"Aw, heck, get it together, soldier."

When he raised his face, the Wolf that had appeared during his first combat mission leaned against the opposite wall, gray-furred arms crossed.

Channing wiped his mouth clean with one sleeve. "I thought I got rid of you."

The Wolf shrugged, dark eyes watching him. "That's the thing about blowing people up. Has a way of staying with you."

Channing said nothing.

The Wolf pointed a clawed finger at the ceiling. "See that?"

Channing rolled his eyes skyward, pupils narrowing to focus on words scrawled in bold red lettering. NOT BY THE HAIR OF MY CHINNY CHIN CHIN.

Gibberish from a child's fairy tale to anyone else, the words had personal meaning that convulsed through him. Together, they formed a phrase that revealed their authors.

Let me in.

Not by the hair of my chinny chin chin.

The phrase originated as a joke between law enforcement officers – his dad and the three Karnac brothers. Over time, the phrase took on more ominous significance: a warning of impending threat.

"You know what to do," said the Wolf. His tail swished in the shadows.

Channing stood up, steadying himself against the heart rendering loss of it all. "I'm not that man anymore. I left that man in the war."

"Look around, campadre. This ain't Sunday brunch with the queen."

"I'll go to the cops. I'll explain –"

"They are the cops. They own the cops."

True, Channing thought. The three brothers ran a booming criminal enterprise right under the eyes of the law. "I'll go to another city." He gestured to the bodies. "I have evidence."

"So did your dad. Look where that got him. "

"I'll get better evidence. Confessions."

The Wolf was suddenly next to him. "Here's evidence for you: A bloodbath, six dead bodies and a troubled war vet with PTSD who talks to imaginary animals."

Channing's mind reeled, flashing on memories of family meals, birthdays, holidays. A million moments that would never happen again.

The Wolf blew musky canine breath on Channing's face. "They slaughtered your family. Who do you think is next?"

Channing closed his eyes. "My family is...gone." The words fell from his mouth like solid things.

"You have another family," the Wolf whispered. "A family that trained you well."

Even if I go to another state, Channing thought, all the evidence points at me. I'm the one who refused the family business, who scorned the police. I'm the explosives expert. I'm the one whose fingerprints are all over this house...

When Channing reopened his eyes, the Wolf held up his niece's skull in the faded lamplight. "You'll have to take all three out in one night – bang, bam, boom."

"I won't kill them."

"As soon as you hit the first one, the others will come after you full tilt." He tugged his snout toward the ceiling – NOT BY THE HAIR OF MY CHINNY CHIN CHIN.

Channing met the steely-eyed gaze of the Wolf as he finished the code phrase, speaking the final words aloud, a return threat of promised retribution. "Then I'll huff and I'll puff and I'll blow their houses down."

***

It took Channing an hour to gather all the supplies he needed. Now he lay flat on his belly on a bluff overlooking the first, and youngest, Karnac brother's house. The Starter, so called because of his aptitude for starting legitimate businesses to front the family's criminal enterprise.

The air felt thin and cold as Channing reached into his duffle bag to retrieve a damp bandana and a dry trigger mechanism. He pressed the trigger and, down below, the house burst into a fireball of light. A surge of heat blasted his face. Tying the bandana around his neck, Channing shoved to his feet, sprinting down the sloping earth. At the bottom, he yanked the bandana over his mouth as jowls of fire crackled and belched over the house.

He crossed the lawn where shadows wriggled underfoot like a squirming mass of black snakes. Ignoring the silhouettes, he reached the house and kicked in the front door as he drew his semi-automatic pistol, a factory black SIG-Sauer P226.

Two men greeted him in the foyer sporting blackened faces, a charred disc of flesh dangling loosely from the side of one man's head. Channing shot both in the upper left shoulder. The men sunk into a thick bank of smoke, disabled but not quite dead.

Still moving, the room materialized around him in vague geometric shapes. Furnishings appeared and dissolved behind fluttering scrims of smoke. Mounting the stairs, flames curled around him, conspiring with the smoke to obscure the house into generalities of age and style.

A hand grappled him out of the haze. Channing spun into it, brought his arm up and around the neck of his attacker, squeezing as he lowered him to the smoldering floor. An inch off the stairs, the other man elbowed him in the ribs. Channing grunted, letting go as the man scrabbled upward, vanishing into the smoke on the second floor.

The Starter, Channing thought, instantly recognizing the telltale dark complexion and short, stubby build. This man murdered my family. Giving chase, Channing bounded onto the landing in an awkward list, following the dwarfish man into the fog.

Feeling along the landing, his hand brushed a doorknob, the hot steel stinging his fingers. He jerked his hand away, stifling a yelp that would have given away his position. He proceeded after the patter of running feet. Even under the damp handkerchief, the cloud of chemicals billowing through the house made it impossible to breathe. If I don't get out soon, I'm going to die.

Channing entered a bedroom, a master by the sheer size of it, just as a stream of fire spewed at his face. He ducked, glancing up to see flames where his bald scalp had just been.

The Starter came at him again, brandishing a burning lamp in one hand and aerosol can in the other.

Channing leapt out of the way of another current of fire, bringing up his gun. "Stop! I just want –"

The Starter blew more fire at him. Channing faked left, went right, flames grazing his left arm. Hot, searing pain rushed up to his shoulder, sending panicked signals to his brain. Run! He spun, snapping off a shot that missed as he scuttled past The Starter in a semi-crouch, fleeing the room.

Backing down the second floor landing, he stopped beside the door with the hot handle, and waited.

A moment later, The Starter stepped into view, raising the homemade blowtorch. "You are going to burn."

"No. You are."

Grasping the doorknob, he flung the door wide, lurching out of the way as a firestorm roared from the opening, engulfing The Starter. The cop thrashed in a cocoon of fire, rammed into the second floor railing, flipping over it, and plummeted fifteen feet to the living room below.

When The Starter dropped beneath the smoke, Channing stood by the railing, waiting for a sense of justice that did not come.

Instead, he retraced his path through the deteriorating structure, out onto the front lawn, and back up the bluff.

Slipping into the Pontiac, he dumped the duffle bag in the passenger's seat and assessed his wounds. Burn marks sleeved his arms and legs, branded his hand, but otherwise he was okay. The cramped Pontiac highlighted the repulsiveness of his own cooked flesh. He closed his eyes – don't puke, don't puke. In the blackness lay the dog pile of bones at his parent's house, the child-size skull, the dead cop. What have I done?

"One down, two to go."

Channing peeked to see the Wolf lounging next to him, duffle bag on his lap. "You don't look so hot," said the Wolf.

"I didn't mean to kill him."

The Wolf stared out the window of the Pontiac at a plume of smoke rising into the night sky.

"I'm not that man anymore," Channing murmured.

The Wolf swiveled toward Channing, black eyes gleaming. "Whoever you are, you better get moving. The countdown has now really begun. Tick. Tick. Tick."

Twenty miles later, they wound down narrow roads framed by black woods. The second brother's house rose in the distance, a majestic structure of stone and glass.

Glossy moonlight shone from a multitude of reflective surfaces. No insects chirped as Channing parked behind a copse of Bradford Pear trees. No night owls hooted warnings.

The Wolf handed him his gun and a small sonic amplification device from the duffle bag. "Go get 'em, killer."

Exiting the vehicle, Channing maneuvered to a vantage point on the tree-lined path that provided a clear view of the house. Here we go...

Directing the sonic device at the house, he pressed the trigger.

A shrill burst of sound shattered every window in the house simultaneously. Braving the blizzard of glass, he quick-stepped from forest to outer perimeter of the second brother's house.

Lights flicked on in the structure, illuminating gaps between stone columns. The odd luminance gave the appearance of a celestial event somehow transposed from sky to earth.

Channing scaled the outer wall, nearly to the second story window when a voice said, "You."

A pale, lanky man peered down from the roof. The second brother, Channing thought, The Teacher. From below, two gunmen scrambled out of the house with weapons drawn.

Channing rotated on the wall, instinctively retrieving and firing his own weapon in one smooth motion, dropping one of the gunmen with a headshot. The other man zigzagged, returning fire.

Clamoring up the stone face of the house, he took a slug in the upper thigh as he breached the top of the roof. Another stray bullet sizzled past his right ear. Standing on shaky legs, his thigh bleeding, he saw a fist-sized rock hurtle toward his head. He staggered out of the way, losing purchase, leaning backwards and nearly tumbling off the roof. He regained footing as a second stone knocked the pistol from his hand. The gun clattered to the courtyard below.

Under a vine-tangled trellis, The Teacher plucked another stone from his rooftop rock garden. A man-made pond bubbled at his sandaled feet.

"Never cared for guns," The Teacher explained, winding up his next pitch. "Too removed...no feel to them. Rocks have feel."

As he said the second "feel", he heaved the rock across the roof.

Limping, Channing skirted the roof edge. The gunman below lobbed a few shots at him, barely missing, and Channing angled toward the center of the roof.

If I can just get close enough...

"I wish your father had let this all go. We were family once." The Teacher picked up another stone.

Channing inched closer. Almost there...

The Teacher flung the stone with such quickness that Channing didn't have time to sidestep it. The rock conked him in the ribcage.

Channing faltered backward, another rock taking out his left knee. He fell hard to the roof.

The Teacher strolled toward him, tossing a stone from hand to hand. "I am not without compassion. I will give you a moment to make peace with your higher power."

Channing clasped his ribcage with a deep moan, exaggerating the injury, and closed his eyes in faux prayer. This is my only chance. I have to turn the tables on him.

When he heard The Teacher's sandals scrape into striking range, Channing opened his eyes, sweeping the man's legs out from under him. The Teacher collapsed to the surface of the roof with a grunt, fumbling the stone. Both men went for the earthy weapon, locking bodies.

Channing arced his back, torqueing his midsection, reaching out for the stone. His fingers found the granite bludgeon, hefting it even as The Teacher forced the two of them to their feet with surprising strength, shoving them toward the edge of the roof.

Panicked, Channing tried to unfasten himself, but the lanky man's grip proved too powerful. The two men accelerated across the roof.

Channing twisted. Come on ... Three feet from the edge of the roof, he tightened his own grip – If I'm going over, we're both going over – using their shared momentum to thrust the two of them airborne.

Gravity took over. The two men nose-dived down the 30-foot drop, each struggling for position. The Teacher screamed in his ear. Channing bucked against him.

Bracing for impact, Channing jogged to the left, swaying an inch, then two, as the momentum carried him in an agonizingly slow rotation, until he swung up and over The Teacher.

Slamming into the earth, The Teacher absorbed the brunt of the collision. He cried out, his scream thinning to a rasping whimper.

Channing rolled off the other man, a staccato throbbing in his chest. When he glanced over, he saw the tip of a stone emerging from The Teacher's belly like the deformed gray scalp of an alien.

The Teacher's milky eyes met his. Blinked. His lips parted as if to speak, but only blood poured out. Channing had witnessed enough soldiers bleeding out on the battlefield to know the man was beyond saving. The Teacher's eyelids sagged shut.

When he no longer heard The Teacher breathing, Channing negotiated to his knees.

A furry paw jutted into view. He took it, and the Wolf helped him to his feet, saying only, "The other thug must have bailed," as Channing staggered drunkenly back to his car. He climbed into the front seat and started the ignition. The Wolf remained quiet as they drove out of the woods.

Halfway to the last brother's house, Channing pulled to the side of the highway. He wrapped his thigh with the bandana to control the bleeding from where he had been shot. He took the next 15 minutes to strap 300 pounds of explosives to the vehicle. Less than two to set the timer for 30 minutes.

"No OFF switch," the Wolf commented. "I like your style."

Restarting the Pontiac, Channing merged onto the Interstate.

***

Rounding the final turn to the third and oldest Karnac brother's house, Channing hit the brakes. Vehicles snaked up the street to the steel fortress of a structure. Bright multi-colored lights strobed into the sky as dance music blared against the night.

My last chance to avenge my family.

Easing to a stop between two black SUVs, he glanced at the dashboard clock. Ten minutes had elapsed since he rigged the Pontiac with explosives. That means I have 20 more minutes...

Channing snatched the duffle bag and stepped out of the Pontiac into the narrow tube of a silenced handgun. The third brother, known as The Accountant, stood in front of him. Built like a boxer, the salt-and-pepper stubble padding both sides of his face made him look more like an aging Hollywood actor than a criminal mastermind.

"Hello, Channing. Something tells me this is going to be the most memorable family reunion yet."

With striking efficiency, The Accountant seized the duffle bag and steered him through a gate, down a series of footpaths lined with exotic plants, to the rear of the house where a single wooden chair squatted on a lakeside pier.

A high fence shielded any view of the house, yet music pulsated into Channing's bones. I'm probably less than 100 yards from a throng of partygoers.

The Accountant nudged him along with the nose of the pistol. "Have a seat."

Channing lowered himself to the chair. The Wolf stood impotently to the side, clawed hands curled at his hips, both of them gazing out over endless dark water in which all hopes seemed to drown.

Channing's wrists were forcibly held together and restrained with a zip tie, securing him to the chair.

The growl of a car engine jerked his attention back to the moment. He gawked as his Pontiac appeared and parked 20 yards down the pier.

My car? What's going – The bombs! There's only 5 minutes left on the timer, and at this range... His heart leaped in his chest.

The Accountant stepped into view as a man in a dark suit climbed out of the vehicle and headed in their direction, carrying a steaming carafe.

"I killed them."

"Say again?"

"I killed them both," Channing repeated. Let it sink in. Let it hurt.

A smile slowly crept over The Accountant's chiseled square of a face. Instead of improving his appearance, the grin twisted it into something grotesque. His black pupils regarded Channing with something akin to fascination.

"I suppose you'd like me to shed a tear for my poor, dead brothers? It was more than I could have asked for really. You outdid yourself." He motioned to the man in the suit who handed him a thick glove, like an industrial oven mitt. He slipped it over his left hand.

Channing stared, dumbfounded.

"Oh, don't look so shell shocked. Who do you think orchestrated all of this?" He waved the gloved hand in the air.

The other man opened the steel carafe, and steam poured out like miniature white flags waving between them.

"At first I was just going to kill them myself, but then I thought, why not let you do that for me? You get revenge while eliminating my competition. Win win." He reached into the steaming carafe with the gloved hand, removing a smooth stone tinted pink with heat.

2 minutes...I have to do something.

"Don't get me wrong," said the Accountant. "I want you to die, but not before you suffer. After all, they are my brothers." He pressed the flat surface of the stone against Channing's left ear.

Pain erupted on the side of his face. "Ahhhhhhhhh!"

"I could have killed you anytime. But that would be far too easy. Your family must pay for trying to take down my empire."

The stone seared a path from his ear to his cheek. No. No. No. Wrenching his head back and forth, his flesh melting. Screaming, screaming.

"Tomorrow morning, when your car is pulled from the lake with your body inside, every news channel in the country will label you a cold-blooded killer," continued The Accountant, moving the hot stone to Channing's forehead. "A psychopath who took the war home with him. Slaughtered his own family and then came after mine."

Someone dunked his head in a furnace. Heat blisters bubbled then popped along his jawline. A skillet shoved against his open mouth, the ridge of his gums, his tongue.

"You will get all of the blame and I all the glory for stopping your murderous rampage. Ironic, huh?" The Accountant laughed.

Channing's eyes widened against the throbbing, melting heat. The clock in his head ticked down to less than a minute.

The Accountant whispered into his undamaged ear. "How does it feel to have your house blown down?"

Five seconds…Channing summoned all his strength for one last desperate effort. Hope to God I'm right. He lunged forward, past The Accountant as the Pontiac detonated.

Everything went black and silent as the force of the blast hurled him into the lake. A heavy solid object landed on his back – maybe debris from the car –as he sunk beneath the surface still tied to the chair.

Coiling his body, he tried to wriggle free, but the chair seemed mostly intact.

A meaty fist struck him in the face. The Accountant. I can see again! He fended off the underwater attacker with a series of scissor kicks, his throat constricting as the erratic movements used up oxygen in his lungs.

Panicked, Channing leveled another lunging foot, catching The Accountant in the gut. He doubled over, then retreated, clawing his way to the surface. Channing flipped over, planted both feet on the bottom of the lake and shoved upward.

When his face finally broke the surface, he inhaled greedily, the weight of the chair already sinking him again. From the corner of his eye, The Accountant grinned madly. "Huff and puff," he said, cackling, waving one arm and then swimming off.

Dropping past the waterline, he shifted his gaze to the pier, now a smoldering mess. The bodyguard lifted a small round object from the duffle bag.

Grenade.

He slipped beneath the surface as the grenade plopped into the water next to him. Wheeling, he swished his legs furiously, the movement creating a current that moved him away from the bomb.

The blast propelled him sideways, under the pier. Shaken, already running low on oxygen again, he tried his restraints. Loosened, but not undone.

Another grenade exploded near him, sending him head first into one of the wooden poles holding up the pier. His head cracked against the beam. Spinning, he raked his wrists against the pole, blindly seeking a sharp surface with which to cut the zip tie.

A third grenade hit the water and Channing scooted away, managing only a few yards before it discharged. The crushing force boomeranged him deeper into the lake. He blinked, vision unfocused.

An arm looped around his throat, tightening. The Accountant, coming in for the kill.

Channing bucked, pitching his head back, skull shattering nose cartilage. The arm slackened.

Then sharp agony from his back. He turned in the water, facing The Accountant, who swung at him again with a hunk of metal. This time Channing shifted himself out of the way.

The Accountant poked one arm above the waterline, waving at his bodyguard to lob more grenades at Channing's position.

No way I'll survive another hit.

Channing shook his head. Not by the hair of my chinny chin chin. He rolled forward, head over chair, coming up behind The Accountant. Bringing both knees up to his chest, he punted the other man, knocking him toward the pier, into the line of fire.

The Accountant's face registered terror as three grenades splashed into the water around him.

All three exploded at once, swallowing The Accountant in shimmering light. A whorl of bubbles rippled outward, pushing Channing further out into the lake.

Near passing out, he finally broke free of the chair and zip tie, climbing to the surface of the water, where he lay on his back, floating and staring up at the night sky rife with stars. Sirens and other emergency vehicles now replaced the dance music.

Floating beside him, the Wolf pushed a hunk of metal across the water between them. "I guess this is finally goodbye, campadre."

Channing clutched the car part, knowing to hold onto it meant drowning in the lake. Still so much left to do, he thought. Bury my family. Prove my innocence. Rebuild my life.

"You were right," added the Wolf. "You aren't that man anymore. You are a better man."

"Goodbye, Wolf."

Channing let go, releasing the car part to the depths. As he did, something peculiar happened, and he thought it awfully strange that a blown up chunk of jumbled mess could bring so much peace.

Puss in Boots

by G.L. Giles

My life changed with a blip. Well, that's how I'd describe it
simply. It was really an anomalous light source detected on my well-
used PT telescope. I belonged to a group of scientists arguably
open-minded enough to actively search for extra-terrestrial life in
the universe. We considered ourselves Paleocontact Theorists;
hence, the PT. As my telescope had a pulse-detection system,
whatever the 'light anomaly' was it looked like it was heading
directly for the bucolic ocher-colored Georgia clay covering most of
my backyard. Furthermore, it looked like there wasn't much time
to prepare for it – maybe five minutes top! Hastily, I pushed aside
the coffee-stained blueprints I'd drawn to aid me in building my
cosplay 'castle' – from the notes I'd taken from a manga entitled
Princess Kookla and Her Bloodbathed Court. It was about a
seductive princess, who, with the help of her lust-ridden prince,
defeats an evil ogre – definitely not the stuff of children's fairy
tales and/or mainstream manga, as the arguably over-the-top gore
factor and sexual situations made it for adults only.

Unfortunately, I'd run out of time to complete the entire castle,
but at least I'd managed to build the front, as a rock-climbing
castle wall, which would be able to sustain my weight in the
cosplay contest reenactment. Also included in the piles of paper
was a flier for the upcoming Diamond City Cosplay Convention in
Macon, Georgia – about two hours away from my remote location. I
brushed aside more papers – including a design for a special-
polymer-soled shoe I planned on perfecting and patenting soon.

Only problem was: my polymer concoction itself. It still didn't stick to surfaces, like rocks, as I had envisioned. So, it still was far from marketable. I hurriedly cleared the clutter from my desk, knocking off the well-worn copy of Zecharia Sitchin's Genesis Revisited, as I was sure I'd left the letter opener under all the items I was currently working on. Though not the best defense, I felt that the letter-opener could function as a makeshift knife on whomever or whatever was about to touch ground in my backyard.

No further proof was needed when I heard a reverberating "Boom!" Almost immediately after that, I felt my home shake. It had never done that in the five years I'd lived there, even during really horrific thunderstorms. In fact, it reminded me of the sonic booms I'd heard from time to time at the airshows I'd attended in south Georgia. That is, before restrictions were put on supersonic aircrafts' flight. Running down the stairs, rather foolishly with the letter-opener-turned-weapon in my hand, I imagined the soon-to-be rapacious destruction of my landlord's backyard. The only obstacle standing between me and the crisp Georgia air of late October was a torn screen door. In my impatience, I could barely baby it with its constant demand of having to be lifted slightly to be opened, as its wooden frame had buckled with age and was especially warped at the bottom. My landlord knew my challenging financial situation, so he didn't charge me much rent to begin with and had never raised it over the years, so I wasn't going to complain to him about little inconveniences. Using my worn-out right running shoe, doctored with both duct tape holding it together and my polymer-formula on its formerly communion-wafer-thin soles, I scooted it under the door to prop it up so that I could exit. I scrimped in many areas to enable me to go to cosplay conventions and work on my polymer soles. So what if I didn't have new shoes or a 'real' Princess Kookla to go with my cosplay display? I'd bought a pressboard rendering of her and the ogre. They'd suffice, as the judges would get the idea. Glancing up, as I exited the weathered screen door, I couldn't even fathom how remotely possible it was that the blip I'd seen on my screen now looked like it was going to crash in my own backyard. Seriously, what were the odds on that?! And, yet, there it was: a grey disc rolling in an erratic stream of red-hot flames about 100 yards out and above. I wasn't sure if it were fear or excitement mounting, as I headed down the well-worn wooden stairs. The boom I'd heard before must've been a sonic boom, as the aircraft was entering our atmosphere.

I was isolated at my country place, but the light and sparks, emitted from whatever was about to land, were blindingly bright. Pretty sure anyone paying attention to the night sky within at least a 20 mile radius would have noticed, even though the inky sky was dissipating fast, as the first rays of dawn tore through it. Must've been about 5:50 a.m. when the vessel crashed. The grey metallic craft, to be more precise, hit the ground hard. Then it became so deeply lined with gashes infused with dingy Georgia clay, as it slid on its erratic trajectory, that it appeared more ocher-colored. It continued sliding – tilted on its right side – until it finally stopped by slamming into an ancient oak tree. The majestic tree had weathered many storms in its over two hundred years of life, but the disruptive vessel that had plowed into it was its death, evinced by the large gashes, like mortal sword wounds, across the base of its trunk. I was a big believer in honoring Mother Nature, so even the polymer I had fabricated for the soles of my shoes was earth-friendly. The soles would have already had the grip I was looking for if I'd been willing to use harmful chemicals, but I was not willing to get ahead at the expense of our Mother Earth. So, I was angry for a second at the pillaging of the grand old tree, even cursing a bit under my breath with, "Damn, man-made technology sometimes sucks." Until I realized that there was a good chance that the alien-to-me craft may very well not be "man-made."

So, when I saw a door, not unlike the door to my older brother's Lamborghini Aventador, open and one fashionable-looking-cuffed-over-the-knee-sepia-colored boot emerge, perhaps I wasn't really that surprised. Perhaps more surprised at the haute-couture fashion. Yet even my internal dialogue was left speechless, for there, before my very eyes, was a feline of about five feet tall! So, a really tall well-outfitted cat started making his way towards me – actually walking on his back legs! With his fine boots, he stepped agilely over the clay grooves dug by his spaceship. I was handling the whole situation remarkably well, I think, until he waved to me with, "Greetings, Jet, your father's sent me here to help you." It was only then that I felt my knees buckle and my consciousness fade. Fortunately, the Georgia clay was still autumn-pliable, so my face and body planted softly into it.

I awoke to the sensation of guitar strings sweeping across my face, caused by the enormous cat's whiskers. Above them, luminous golden eyes stared down at me anxiously. Startled, I sat up as quickly as I could. It dawned on me that it was somewhat humorous that I was going to the cosplay competition as Princess Kookla's hero: the 'Marquis of Catanova', also known as Jetavi Dorngolden. I felt a special kinship with the hero, as my own name was Jet.

The talking cat brought me back to the moment with, "Are you alright?"

"Yes, I guess so," I began, but before I could say more, we were both startled by a bright light in the sky and a loud boom. "Sonic boom?" I realized the moment the words escaped my lips just how ludicrous it was that I was actually asking a huge furry feline the question.

So, adding to my new bizarre reality, or the psychotic break that I could have just as easily been experiencing, the obviously intelligent cat replied, "Probably, as the craft is most likely travelling faster than the speed of sound, so—"

"Shock waves," I said, finishing his sentence. I didn't have time to question how the strange talking cat knew my name or why he'd referenced my deceased father, as the more pressing concern of another UFO about to land not too far away was taking center stage in my mind. Fortunately, the second one wasn't going to land in my backyard.

I looked at the finely clad feline. His boots weren't his outfit's only designer feature. He also wore what might be considered pantaloons and a long-sleeved poet's shirt that billowed where sleeves of that sort should and tapered at his waist thanks to a thick belt he wore. In fact, he almost looked like a gentleman pirate – except for the fact he was feline and came from a spaceship. I saw with some amazement that he didn't look surprised at the other flying disc making its way across the sky. Not that I was exactly an expert in reading the facial expressions of a big talking cat, but I didn't see any of his whiskers twitching or anything like that, so I took it to mean that he was expecting whatever was about to crash – maybe 30 miles away from where we were in my backyard.

"Great gods," the cat said in a gravelly low voice, "I didn't think an Annunorcus would be landing here this soon. We'll have to leave – soon!"

"W–w–wait a minute," I stammered. "What the hell is an Annunorcus?" I asked, already feeling an inexplicable fear rise in the pit of my stomach.

"What the hell, indeed! Annunorci are the product of the snake-like aliens, the Annunaki females to be precise, mating with Orcus, the ogre-like god of his planet's underworld."

"You mean, like the Annunaki, who favor human enslavement? And, like people-eating ogres?"

"And, cats!" the large feline volunteered with a bristling of his fur, and then added, "They give the zombicarns, your zombies, a run for their money! And, the zombicarns are their only known natural enemy. Even worse, an Annunorcus can shapeshift into a snake when it feels threatened, so they can make themselves small enough to go undetected."

"Disgusting! Mostly the part about eating humans and cats." Then, after pausing for a minute to let the information digest, I asked, "How can they be stopped?"

"Leave that to me," the cat said with a knowing look.

"But, why is the Annunorcus here, and is there just one, or should I say Annunorci?"

"From what I can tell of the relatively small craft that just crashed, it looks like we're in luck and just one Annunorcus was sent. I'll wager he's looking for diamonds and that he's been sent to collect them by the Annunorci League. Unfortunately, he's probably also been instructed to not hesitate to kill anyone who gets in his way. Actually, he naturally does that anyway anytime he gets hungry, and Annunorci are known for their voracious appetites. Again, not unlike a zombie."

"That's funny because Diamond City Con has..."

"The largest selection of natural diamonds in one place at one time," the cat said in a remarkably casual tone of voice considering what we were up against – though he finished my sentence with a solemn look.

Trying to lighten the gravity of the situation, I offered, "but I thought aliens were into mining our gold, not diamonds. You know the story common amongst paleocontact theorists: that they're here to enslave us and make us mine the gold for them."

"Yes, well, maybe some are, but I can assure you that the Annunorci are into diamonds. Your planet's natural diamonds!"

"But, why? I hardly think it plausible that ogres of any sort would want diamonds as a fashion accessory."

At that the large cat kind of purred-spat, which I think was his way of laughing, with, "You've got your father's sense of humor. They have to have the natural kind of diamonds your planet offers, since they depleted their own planet's supply. They use them to keep their many bloody industries functioning. The synthetic diamonds won't do. And, they particularly like the kind found in the famous Diamond Fields of Georgia. Something to do with the Georgia clay producing a softer sandstone where those diamonds are found."

"So, have any other Annunorci landed here in the past?"

"I don't think so, as their presence would be hard to miss, unless—"

"Unless they're at something like a cosplay convention, especially one like Diamond City Con which kicks off their festivities on Halloween," I said, with growing awareness and apprehension.

"Precisely," he said. "Plus, I had intel from my planet that they planned on sending out an Annunorcus tonight."

"I see," I said slowly, nodding my head with as much understanding as my addled brain could manage, "because Diamond City Con is tomorrow!"

"Today...your Halloween is today!" the cat corrected.

"Right," I said slowly, "Diamondween, as some are already calling it, is today. I stand corrected and blame my error on little sleep and an alien space craft with a talking cat landing in my backyard." I glanced down at my wristwatch, which glowed with the lighted numerals reading 6:15. "Diamond City Con doesn't open its doors till 9 a.m., so we still have some time."

"But not much," the intelligent feline added. "You need to gather everything you need together quickly."

So, within ten minutes, I'd packed my tired '72 Ford Pinto to the brim with all my cosplaying paraphernalia – except for the Kookla Castle Climbing wall, as it was too big to fit, so it went in the back of a small U-Haul I'd rented. Wouldn't have been such a tight fit, but I hadn't expected to have a cat companion who took up a good portion of my passenger seat.

As far as my cosplaying re-enactment went, anyone familiar with the popular series would know that I was performing a scene from Book Five, my favorite: Princess Kookla and Her Bloodbathed Court. Critics said that it was too bloody for mainstream manga, but I loved it because of it being the tale of a pauper-turned-marquis-then-prince who saves Princess Kookla by swimming across the moat and climbing the castle wall to rescue her from an ogre. It's of note that Princess Kookla was generally quite able to handle herself, as she'd proved going up against a group of those looking to overthrow her government in Book Three: Princess Kookla Saves Dejahland.

Making good time on the road from my country home to the more metropolitan Macon, Georgia (where Diamond City Con was taking place), we didn't say much the first half hour of the drive, but we did get some strange looks directed towards my furry companion in the passenger seat. I might have enjoyed the stares, if the threat of an 'ogre' about to crash Diamond City Con weren't real. So, instead of smiling at my passenger later on, I crankily said, turning towards him with a frown, "Please do me a favor and drop the bit about how my dad sent you here to help me. That's bullshit...my dad's been dead for over five years!"

Looking at me with a sideways glance, the cat, whose real name I still didn't know, offered coolly, "So, because your father has passed from your world, you think he's dead?"

"No shit, Sherlock," I couldn't help replying. I tended to be a smartass when trying to mask my fear. "I don't know about where you're from, but dead here means that those who've died can no longer speak."

"Your father is perhaps dead in your world, but not in my dimension. You see, it's not so much that I'm from another planet as it is I'm from another dimension, comprenez-vous?"

"Well, just supposing that I believe you, then why did my father send you to me, and not to my two older brothers?"

"Ah, now you're starting to ask the right questions! Let me start with properly introducing myself: Je suis Le Maitre Chat ou Le Chat Botté. On my planet, in my dimension, French is the common language. So, I am formally known as 'Puss in Boots', or 'The Master Cat', but you can call me Matt."

"Really? 'Matt the Cat'? I feel like I'm in a bad Dr. Seuss book with a multi-lingual feline!"

At that, Matt kind of purr-snorted with, "I see you've got your father's wonderful sense of humor."

"Yeah, he was funny alright," I said with a mixture of both hurt and longing. "So funny that he left me absolutely 'nada' in his will."

"You sure about that?" Matt asked.

"Well, yeah. My oldest brother inherited his numerous houses and land, and my middle brother received all his possessions — including all his 'mules'."

"Mules?" the overgrown cat queried.

"Yeah, you know, his 'mules with a lot of horsepower,' as in his silver Shelby SSC Aero, green Bugatti Veyron, et cetera."

Looking at me quizzically, the cat offered, "So, you think he left you nothing?"

"Well, the proof's in the pudding, or the lack of it, in this case," I replied. I had racked my brain for over five years about what in the world I'd done to fall so out of his favor.

Looking at me with another sideways glance, Matt offered, "Well, what if I were to tell you that your father left you something even better than what your brothers inherited?"

"I'd say you were a crazy furball because he left me NOTHING."

"Except..." Matt paused dramatically, "ME!"

"So, let me get this straight: my dead father isn't really dead. Rather, he's living in a different dimension with talking cats, AND he took over five years to get my inheritance to me, and it's a CAT – no offense."

"None taken."

"Look, I'm too hungry to wrap my head around all this right now, and I'm gonna need some fuel to set up my cosplay display. We have about 15 minutes' leeway. Wanna get some breakfast? What do you eat? Our drive-thrus don't serve filet of mouse or lizard or anything like that," I said in a somewhat sarcastic tone, but I almost immediately gave him a sheepish sideways glance, as I hadn't really meant to be that rude.

"My dear boy, we have long since evolved from being meat eaters. Do you think that humans are the only species who have a choice in whether or not to eat meat?! I can assure you that more felines on my planet are vegetarians than humans on yours. Not to say that we can't eat meat, it's just that most cats where I'm from find it repugnant."

A few minutes later, we were munching on the cheese biscuits we'd gotten from a drive-thru. We didn't say a word more to each other for the rest of the drive. I broke the silence, after pulling in a parking spot for vendors and cosplay competitors, with, "Do you think you could help me carry some of my stuff in?"

"Of course," was all Matt said. We unloaded the cosplay items onto a large dolly and then got a badge for Matt, as I already had one. Then, we hurried past the vendors' rooms. There must've been at least 20 rooms on either side of the hallways set up just for those selling their wares, and if it'd been another time, I would have spent hours just browsing the action figures, books, graphic novels, comics, et cetera.

"With any luck, the Annunorcus hasn't arrived yet," I said, right before Matt and I rolled our dolly with my Kookla display past the last of the vendor rooms. I was reminded that it was also Halloween (Diamondween), as some people dressed as simply zombies, not even the cosplaying kind, almost swerved into the dolly as we entered the atrium. Momentarily annoyed and briefly thinking that they had about the brains of true zombies, I shot them an 'eat shit' glance, but then focused on a more pressing concern with, "Maybe he had a hard time finding transportation after his space vessel landed?"

"With any luck," Matt responded.

Even the Annunorcus wasn't front and center in my mind when we entered the atrium, for the already heavily guarded area was ablaze with the reflection of the diamonds displayed under the skylight. In fact, I was so fixated on the sparkling gems that I almost ran my dolly into a pretty lady about my age.

"Excuse me," she said politely, glancing with some amusement at the dolly, as she herself was dressed up as Princess Kookla, and all I had was the crude representation. "Book Five?" she asked with some amusement, for it was fairly well-known that most guys preferred that one.

I felt my palms get sweaty, but I managed to get out without stuttering, "And, you, with that gown...showcasing your ample breasts (I thought, somewhat salaciously)...Book Three?"

"Yes," she answered, with a smile that showcased her dimples. "I guess we're kinda predictable, huh? Girls and our love of Book Three?"

"Yeah," I offered, with a smile.

"Maybe we should collaborate next time, as it looks like together we'd have had it in the bag." Then switching her attention to Matt, she said with appreciation, "Great prosthetics!"

"Thank you," Matt graciously replied. But before the 'Princess' could take a closer look, added, "Ahem, Jet, we need to get going."

Looking at the 'Princess' with an apologetic glance, I proclaimed, "Guess he's really vested in my winning."

No sooner had we gotten to the long stage in the back (where all cosplayers competing were setting up) than we heard screams coming from the atrium. "Looks like the Annunorcus has arrived,"

Matt said grimly. "You finish setting up, and I'll attend to him. Oh, but before I go – take these," he offered, slipping off his fine boots and handing them to me. "They are scientifically engineered to fit any size foot, and they have a special polymer sole – like what you've been searching for, so they'll aid you in climbing your castle wall. You didn't think they were just superfluous, did you? Besides, I'm quicker on all fours," he said, quickly bounding away.

Unlike most cosplay competitions, all contestants were all set up on the stage against the back wall, and fortunately, the Kookla I'd met was set up next to me. I learned her real name was Etta – short for Elisetta. Strangely undeterred by the chaos in the atrium, all the judges still planned on making their rounds.

The judges got to my display first, and I was happy to perform with no glitches, as Matt's boots clung to my rock climbing wall display incredibly well. The judges gave a nod to me for a job well done…that was up to the point that Matt came bounding across the stage with a deadly Annunorcus chasing him.…

***

It would have been wonderful if everything had turned out peachy. After all, we were in the state of Georgia, but, unlike many faerie tales, real life tends to get a bit messy. So, in short, the Annunorcus tore into one of the judges in front of Etta's Kookla Display, spewing so much gore and viscera about that one of the other judges slid in it. And, the Annunorcus would have consumed more, if I hadn't had the presence of mind to rope those humans I'd seen dressed up as zombies earlier into scaring the Annunorcus, who thought them Zombicarns, into changing into a snake (as Zombicarns prefer large prey). Then, Matt was able to pounce on him and devour him! Turns out, though generally a vegetarian cat, he would still eat ogre-snake meat if it meant saving all of humanity! Due to the gruesome circumstances, nobody won the competition. Yet, I did leave Diamond City Con with Etta's digits as well as with Matt, who talked incessantly on the ride home about my patenting the earth-friendly formula in his boots, so I felt that somehow financial freedom wasn't far behind.

The Fat and the Fire

by Georgia L. Jones

Deep in the woods of the Ozarks hills lies a hollow mouth carved into the mountainside by the gods and devils of old. Most men don't go near it, although they don't know why. The chills that run down their spines tell them to step the other direction. The place is hallowed ground for the spirits of evil and death, of immorality and greed. It will pull the very heart from your chest, given the chance, and leave you to rot in the fallen leaves... until the mouth itself awakens, birthing a witch so evil that her spell draws you in. Then she eats you, but not until she tortures you with fat and fire.

***

"Don't you understand there is nothing left? Hell, I can barely feed us now. If things get any worse, I don't know what we're going to do. You should count your blessings that we have a warm home to stay in, instead of constantly bitching about what we don't have."

He knew Susan had been accustomed to the finer things in life and he was thankful that she had helped him with the kids after Jane died five years ago. He would never love her like the kids' mom, but he had always done his best to take care of her wants, even before his own needs. He also knew that hard times tend to bring out the worst in people. Susan wasn't immune to hard times' worst effects. She had always been somewhat selfish, but she was his wife, and he would stand by her.

Now, the banks had closed, the government had crumbled, and the animals were all infected from the alien meteor that had crashed to earth a year ago. It was every man for himself. The economic hardship had taken its toll on many. The weakest had taken their own lives. The rest were just trying not to starve.

Sitting at the table, he dropped his head into his hands as tears welled in his eyes. He was a macho kind of guy, and now he couldn't provide for his family as he had always done. He had to think of something. Anger gripped him as he realized the wetness dripping down his cheek. He jumped to his feet and hurriedly went out to the woodpile that he had been working on. His mind ran wild with anger as he swung the maul again and again. After each heavy swing, he threw the split wood toward the pile.

They didn't have enough of anything to go around. People couldn't buy wood with money anymore and hadn't for quite some time. Of course, the money did little good anyway these days. Flour, wheat, and corn were so scarce that they weren't even willing to part with that in trade for a warm night most of the time, but occasionally they had no choice.

Hans, a spindly and weathered sixteen-year-old, made a fleet-footed dash around the house at the sound of the wood-splitting. He could tell his father was angry by the pace at which the maul hit the wood and had learned, in these instances, to tread lightly.

He grabbed his own maul and began working a few yards from his father. He could see the red, fierce concentration in his eyes and looked away quickly. He remembered all too well his mom and how she could always quell his dad's anger, but Susan could do no such thing. As a matter of fact, she seemed to inspire it.

Hans swung strike for strike with his father, and neither spoke a word. He knew what was troubling the man. Everyone knew what was troubling everyone—the hunger, the disease, the hardship of this lifetime. They simply worked, swinging their mauls, until Susan yelled that the corn mush was on the table.

"Come and get it, you shit-bred heathens!"

Hans glanced at his father out the corner of his eyes and couldn't help but ask. "Dad, why do you let her talk to us that way?"

He could feel the anger swell out of his father and ducked too late. His father's hand landed on the back of his head like a hammer thumping short and quick, making Hans stumble forward.

"She is my wife and I will NOT have you talking that way. She has had it just as rough as the rest of us in the last few years. If she's a little moody, just consider that she has a husband, a mouthy sixteen-year-old boy, a hormonal thirteen-year-old girl, and her own woman things that she is dealing with. You are lucky she cooked you dinner!"

Hans looked straight into his eyes and screamed back at him.

"You mean WE'RE lucky that she has anything to cook. I'm sick of all this, too, but Grace and I aren't allowed to complain. We aren't allowed to have an opinion. This is bullshit dad and you KNOW IT!"

This was the first time that Hans had ever raised his voice to his father in such a manner, and he had already braced himself, expecting a much harder blow. He knew he could take it. He was about to explode with his own anger. Anger at his step-mom who had no respect for his sister or himself, but also anger at his father who had stood aside and let all of this happen.

"If you don't like it, you can leave. Go on out there with the animals, see how long you last."

Hans looked towards the ground because he knew his father was right. The only choice he had was to put up with Susan. He wouldn't survive out there alone for one night and honestly was scared to try, by far more scared of the woods than of his stepmother.

Dinner was somber as each of them slowly ate the corn mush that, mounded together, wasn't enough for one. Nobody spoke a word except Grace, who, after she had eaten, only said, "Thank you stepmother." She spoke softly, as she had heard the argument between Hans and her father, and she didn't want to stir the proverbial pot.

***

Late that night, Grace awoke and heard talking downstairs. She crept out her door to find Hans with a finger to his lips. They stood in the upstairs hall to hear their father and stepmother talking about them.

"You could always drug them both and load them into the wagon. You could take them as far out in the woods as you can go in a half day and drop them there. You should go south. They surely wouldn't be able to find their way home."

Somewhere, long ago, Susan had heard the stories of a witch that lived in a cave deep in the south woods. If the stories were true and the witch actually ate children to appease a curse, then she would gladly offer Hans and Grace to her. She would do anything to end this God-Forsaken curse on their lives.

Grace grasped Hans's hand in an effort to hold back the tears. She couldn't believe Susan was actually talking about getting rid of them. Why wouldn't they just kill them? She knew the answer to that when her father responded.

"I don't know Susan; I think we can make this work. Hans is getting bigger and stronger. His mind isn't that of a child anymore. He can help me chop wood, and maybe we can sell it for food soon, and Grace will be finding a man before much longer."

Susan knew that the children's father would never be talked into killing them, but dumping them off? Possibly. He would think they had a chance of survival on their own.

"If I had arsenic, I would take care of the problem myself, but since I don't, you better do something. They are growing too quickly, they eat too much, and it won't be long before Hans takes over the household, and with his temper, he will destroy us. I heard your argument with him today. He hates me and I know he will try to kill me sooner or later."

"He would never—"

Susan interrupted his sentence. "Oh, he would, and I think you know it. Besides, if they stay, we will all four lie right here and die. Better they have a chance out there and we have a chance here to live, all of us."

"Do we have any of the Propofol left?" As the words came out of his mouth, he felt the surreal feeling of being beaten, and it came through in his voice. "I won't be taking them south though; we will go north."

He, too, had heard legends of a witch, and whereas he didn't necessarily believe them, he didn't want to take any chances.

Hans looked at Grace and whispered, "Act like we don't know anything. I will take care of this, Grace. I will take care of you, for God will not forsake us in this time of need."

They both went to their rooms and didn't sleep because of the conversation they had heard. Grace lay in her bed and cried all night, knowing that tomorrow she must rise with a smile and pretend that she didn't know that she truly wasn't wanted.

Hans was busy making a plan. He knew that he wasn't a child anymore. If they were to make it through this alive, he needed to grow up and take care of his baby sister. He got up and quietly dug through the closet, which held only a few items because everything else had been sold off before things had gotten really bad.

He found the box quickly. It held the jacks that his mom had played with him as a young child. He had convinced his dad that it was a good thing to keep just in case they needed the metal from them later. He must have forgotten about them, or he was just being generous by letting him keep one thing that harbored happy memories of family. He wasn't sure which it was, and now it really didn't matter. He was hoping they would save their lives tomorrow. In the early morning hours, he filled the pockets of his jacket with them and carefully put them together so they wouldn't jingle.

***

The next morning when Hans went downstairs, his father was already out chopping wood. Susan was stirring corn mush over the fire and looked around with a sweet, deceitful grin. Hans grinned back at her with a bit of a spiteful gleam in his eye.

"Hans darling. Breakfast is nearly ready." Susan did seem very cheerful this morning.

"That's okay, you all share it. I'm going out to help dad." He hadn't passed up a meal for longer than he could remember, but then again, Susan hadn't called him darling – ever, so it was even.

Susan winced at him as though he had thrown a dagger through her.

"You won't get anymore today if you don't eat now. This will be all of it." Her voice sounded hollower than it had, and the smile had faded from her face. "Suit yourself."

Hans went out to the woodpile and began splitting wood alongside his father. At one point he looked up to find his father staring at him with an odd smile, one he had never seen before, but inside he could see the sadness in it.

"Dad, you know everything will be okay eventually, don't you?" He swung his own maul maliciously, trying to hide the heartbreak that he was feeling towards him.

"Someday, son, everything will be okay. Never lose sight of God. He will guide you through anything." A sudden happy smile took his face. "You know, you're nearly a man now. You will soon have a wife of your own and a family."

For a moment Hans was happy. He felt his father's love, and he wanted nothing more than to run to him, wrap his arms around his neck, and maybe even jump into his lap as he had as a small child, but that wasn't how men acted. Men just smiled and looked worried a lot, so that was what he did. The one thing his father didn't know was that Hans really was worried. He was worried about Grace, who reminded him so much of his beloved mother. He was also worried about his father and how he would come to grips with himself after plotting such a horrible fate for his children. He held his smile nonetheless.

After a few more pieces of wood had hit the pile, Susan came out the door with two glasses in her hand. The lemon yellow substance that they held was tempting, but Hans knew he couldn't drink it. He wanted to desperately because he was parched from hard work.

"Grace is eating her breakfast and yours, too, Hans. I thought you men might like a tall glass of lemonade. I found one small lemon in the back of the cellar this morning. I saved it for you hard-working men."

Susan sounded so fake that even father had to look at her twice, as if to say, 'you're laying it on a little thick.' She returned to her normal demeanor and added, "Now, get back to work so we can eat again."

Hans tipped his glass up and pretended to take a sip while father drank his to the bottom.

"I will save some for later. It's so good; I just don't want it to end."

He carried his glass to the woodpile and set it down, spilling about a fourth of it onto the ground. After a few minutes, he picked the glass up and again pretended to drink. When setting it down, he spilled part of it on the ground, making certain to give out an "ahh, this tastes great" sound after each supposed sip.

It wasn't long until Hans sat down and pretended to go to sleep. He knew that the drug worked very quickly and didn't want to alert his father to his plan. It worked.

Their father loaded them both onto the wagon and headed into the woods. It wasn't long until Hans began dropping the jacks along the bumpy trail.

After hours of traveling, his father stopped. He bent and gently kissed each one of them on the forehead before even more gently unloading them and setting them by a tree. He knelt before them and prayed silently. Hans knew his father was asking for forgiveness for himself as well as safety for the children. His father turned the wagon and was out of sight in moments.

Hans gently began to shake Grace to wake her, but he would have to wait until the drug wore off, which he knew would take a couple more hours. He didn't want to be in the woods at night, but tonight they would have no choice. They would have to walk through the woods and hope to find their way home before they were found by something hungrier than they were.

When Grace woke, they began their journey home. The next day around noon they arrived, unharmed, unscathed, but hungry as could be. Their father was so happy to see them. As it turned out, the very day he returned home a man had come and bought wood for corn and flour. So, they had enough food after all. Things were looking up.

***

It didn't take long for the feasting to cease. The flour made biscuits and the corn made more mush than they could eat in a meal. They were all in a better mood for a while; even Susan seemed a little more pleasant.

When the food became short again, the good moods stopped, and things were back to what had become normal. Hans once again had the look of a man. He wore a smile and looked as worried as ever. He looked that way because he was worried. He knew that if the food became too short, Susan would once again plot to get rid of them.

Just as he had thought, she did plan it, only this time he didn't learn of it beforehand, and neither did Grace. On a cold day, in the middle of winter, he and Grace woke in the woods.

Had he known, he could have stashed the jacks in his pockets again. Had he known, he wouldn't have eaten or drank anything that day, but he had been tricked well. This time he had no memory of even falling asleep. The last thing he remembered was going out the door after breakfast to cut wood. The poison had been in the mush.

"Don't worry, Grace. I will take care of you. I have walked these woods before and was on this same path not so long ago. We will be home before tomorrow night."

Grace smiled at him because she knew that Hans would take care of her. He would make sure that she made it home safe.

Little did either of them know that this path was not the same path they had taken before. This path was on the south side of the mountain. This path was the one that no man goes down. It was the cursed path. Susan had seen to that.

After walking for hours, and as the sun began to set, they saw the mouth of the cave. It looked like a good place to rest for a while and the smell of something delicious was coming from inside. Hans couldn't quite place it, but he knew the smell from long ago. It was a something that his mother had cooked for them, back before everything changed.

Hans had a hold of Grace's hand as he led her deeper into the cave. Finally, they saw a light flickering in the distance. They quietly walked toward it to see what was making the delicious smell that had both of their stomachs aching with hunger.

Before they could see her clearly, the lady stirring the pot began to speak to them.

"Come on in children. I have your dinner ready. I know you're both very hungry."

Her voice was as sweet as the stew she was stirring and bore a striking resemblance to their own mother. As she turned to hand them a bowl, Hans and Grace both looked startled at one another. This woman looked exactly as their mother had looked. They became quickly entranced with her and began sipping their soup down as though nothing in the world had changed five years ago. They were lost in a time of happiness.

***

When Grace awoke, her first curiosity was where Hans could be. He would have been beside her if he could have. She hadn't remembered falling to sleep, and the rocks on which she was lying were hard, cold, and uncomfortable. She wondered for a moment if it had all been a dream.

She realized quickly it had been no dream when she saw the woman who had reminded them so much of their mother stirring a pot. She was chanting in some foreign tongue as the flames rose and fell to the sound of her words.

"Excuse me ma'am. Where is my brother? I must see him at once."

Grace tried to sound demanding, even with the panic that she felt. Panic quickly turned to horror when the lady turned to her. Her face was covered with peeling skin that looked like she herself had been boiled in the pot that she stirred.

"He is safe, for now. I have locked him up. You must know my intentions."

Her cackle made Grace tremble to the bone with fear. She had heard the legends of the witch that cooked and ate people who wandered into her path. Grace had never believed it was true, not until now. She now knew it was true, and she and Hans were her next victims.

She approached Grace and handed her a bowl of stew that didn't smell near as sweet as the stew they had earlier.

"Take this around that corner and hand it to your brother. You tell him to eat it up, or I will kill you first. If he eats well and gets fat, I will spare you and eat him."

She went around the corner, and Hans was there. The bars that lined the front of the hole were shiny in the flickering firelight from the other room. Grace knew the witch was planning on eating both of them, but she delivered the stew and the message with precision. All the while, she looked to see how to get Hans free from the cell that imprisoned him. She could see that Hans was already larger than he had been when they arrived, and there was no way he could fit between the bars.

She returned to the witch and took her seat on the cold rocks, just as the witch expected.

"There my pretty, now you have a bowl also. You must keep up your strength to help me in my chores."

Grace took her bowl and ate it up. She couldn't help but chuckle inside at the irony of going from a place where she was starving to death to a place where she was eating to death. There was no humor in it, but the irony was almost more than she could contain.

After another sleep, Grace had taken Hans two more bowls of stew and eaten some herself. She was also beginning to become plump. The witch asked her to come and stir the stew while she went out of the cave. Thinking it may be a trick of some sort, Grace stayed with the fire continuously. The last thing she wanted was the witch to be mad at her. She had learned so much in the last five years with Susan; one of those things was how to appease a witch.

After several days of the same routine, Hans had begun to become so plump that he could hardly get to the bars to get his stew. He knew that he had to, though, or the witch would kill Grace. Even if he had to die, he wished for nothing more than his sister to be spared.

Grace, however, had done some thinking of her own. She knew that the witch was also a bit lazy and was depending more on her to do the dirty work. She had brought meat from somewhere and was now having Grace carve it up, start the fire again, and stir the stew.

This day when Grace awoke, she knew it was the day. Somehow she knew that the witch would be preparing to carve up Hans and feed him to them both. When the witch pulled the knife out of her scabbard, she told Grace to get to the fire and get it stoked up high. Grace had no choice but to think quickly. The time had come, and it was now or never.

"Ma'am, I have forgotten the way to stack the wood under the pot. Could you please help me?"

Grace used a calm and humbled tone, and the witch came almost maternally to her side. The witch lay the magic knife down on a stone and turned to lay the wood on the fire, trusting Grace completely. Grace grabbed the knife quickly, and as the witch bent over she began to stab her in the back, where she could only hope there was a heart underneath to pierce.

Sure as the sun would rise another day, the witch fell into the fire and began to burn. The screams that came from the flailing shadows of what remained of her turned the cave into a cavern of unholy terror and shattered the steel that held Hans in his imprisonment.

It took a spell of time to find their way out of the cave, and once they did, they found that grass had begun to grow where only winter's ice and leaves had been.

As they climbed the mountainside through the haze of heavenly fog, an angel appeared to them. Her voice was true, and Grace knew that she was blessed by the God that had given her the strength to save them.

"Grace, you have broken the witch's curse by killing her. You have put her back into the pit from which she came. Is there a joy that you would accept if I bless you?"

"Yes. I would like to restore the world to a better time. I would like for us to not have to worry about such things as food ever again."

In the blink of an eye, before them there was a carriage with a big white horse attached. The horse looked healthy, and when Grace opened the door to the carriage, there was more gold than she could possibly see inside. Hans and Grace climbed aboard the carriage. The stallion stepped proudly into the daylight, carrying them to their doorstep while they watched the healing world around them. Deer scampered through the forest, happy and healthy, chipmunks ran amuck in the thickets of brush, and birds took flight in the air chirping joyfully.

When Hans ran into the house to let his father know they were home and that everything would be okay, he found him sitting at the table with his head in his hands.

"Father, father. We are home and we have a surprise for you."

"Hans." His father jumped to his feet with joy. He grabbed his son and held him tight to him in a hug. "I'm so happy to see you Hans! Where is your sister?"

"She is outside. Where is Susan?"

Hans's father became solemn. "Susan fell ill after I returned home last winter. Winter came and went, and she passed with it."

"We are home now, father, and the world is healing. We have brought more gold than we will ever use with us."

They walked out of the house and saw Grace standing in the yard with a pile of gold larger than any woodpile they had ever cut. They all ran together and fell onto the ground happier than a pigs in shit, forever more.

The Girl in the Red Hood

by Brad Parnell

How did it come to this? What was he doing lying in a
stranger's bed dressed in an old woman's tattered and unpleasant
smelling sleeping gown? Why was he now being accused of
mauling that same old woman to death? His head was spinning
and his stomach churning. His back was against the wall. Never in
his whole life had he been in such a predicament. The wolf thought
things could not have gotten any worse, yet they had. If only he'd
taken his own advice and ignored the little red hooded girl when
he met her in the woods hours earlier. If only he'd seen through
her transparent ruse and ignored her pleas, he might not be in this
most dire of situations. He would give anything to be able to
escape. Yet here he was, staring down the sharp blade of a
woodsman's axe, hoping for some kind of a miracle.

It had begun for the wolf like any other day. He got up with his
pack and milled about to make sure everyone was doing well. The
pack had been on the move recently; with no pups to care for in a
den, they were able to stride about where and when they pleased.
After awhile they began to get hungry, so he had gone off to find
food, minding his own business and sticking to his own territory.
The weather made the day particularly nice, without a cloud in the
bright blue sky. The autumn temperature was crisp and cool.
Before long he caught the scent of a deer, and soon he was hot on
its trail. He knew it was close. He could smell it. Just as he was
about to pinpoint the location, another scent got mixed with the
deer's. It was a strange scent. That's when *she* came into the

picture. At first she seemed like any other hapless moppet skipping down a well-worn trail through the forest. But there was something different about her, and the wolf knew it, but he just couldn't put his paw on it.

For one thing she was traveling through the woods all alone, or so it seemed. He rarely saw people at all in the woods, but seeing little people alone was something new. Oh sure, the wolf had heard other stories of children traipsing about in the forest, but he chalked it up to other animals telling tall tales. He'd heard a tale about two kids out alone who ended up in a gingerbread house and then got eaten by a witch, as if he ever believed that one. The whole idea of a house made out of gingerbread was preposterous. Of course, he also remembered the one the bears always told about the girl with the golden hair who trashed their place. He never figured in a million years he'd be involved in something like that or worse, even if they were true.

This different-seeming moppet looked normal enough for a human. Underneath that big red hood she had dark brown eyes that matched her chestnut hair that flowed down around both sides of her face. The wolf had never seen a human child up close before. He assumed because of her small size she must be fairly young, but now he was having significant doubts. She seemed startled to see the wolf at first, but she didn't seem afraid. That should have been a red flag to the wolf right away: most humans were afraid of wolves. That fear helped keep the balance of nature, yet she had no fear at all. She walked right up to him, slowly at first, but once she realized he wasn't running away, she moved with less caution. She was far too relaxed.

At this point he knew it was too late to get away. He didn't know what to do. He hadn't been this close to a human before and certainly hadn't prepared any conversational material. She gave a little wave and said "hello". The wolf responded in kind, and the conversation began. They spoke of the good weather and the beauty of the forest. The next thing the wolf knew, she was telling him his yellow eyes were beautiful. She said they were soulful and that she could get lost in his gaze if she were not careful. At this his heart skipped a beat. He wasn't used to such talk, especially not from a young human girl.

She carried a basket with her, and the wolf never thought to check it out. He took the little hooded girl's word that the basket was filled with treats for her grandmother. After all, why would she lie about it? She told him that her grandmother had been down in the dumps and that she wanted to take her some treats to cheer her up. According to the girl, the old woman had been through some tough times recently and had been kind of lonely. She didn't have a lot of friends and family around, and visiting her was the least the girl could do.

The wolf never thought to ask why her grandmother lived so deep in the forest where so few humans dared to reside. Looking back, that should have been another red flag – that, and of course the idea that her parents would let her travel alone to visit her grandmother in such a place. He wished he'd questioned her a little more. Maybe then he wouldn't be in this mess. No, he thought – he wished he'd never seen her face at all. He knew everything would have been different if he hadn't.

That face, that sweet, innocent looking face, that was able to make him believe the most outlandish fabrications. He'd been warned about trusting such faces, but he never believed he would run into one. He imagined that when they were handing out cute, this girl would have been in front of the line and then came back for seconds. Was it her rosy cheeks or the cute dimples that stood out the most? No, it was her eyes, those big brown eyes with the fluttering eyelashes, that had made him feel funny. He didn't quite know how to explain it, but it was something he'd never felt before. His instinct was telling him to flee, but the longer he stayed and listened to the girl talk, the longer he stared into those eyes, the stranger he felt. It was almost as if his common sense had taken a fast train out of town without even buying a ticket.

On the surface he knew the story she gave him about her grandmother enjoying practical jokes didn't seem right, but it could have been. How was he to know? He'd heard all kinds of stories about humans and their foolish ways. Then the idea was presented to take part in a joke to help entertain the old woman. Initially he thought the idea rubbish, but she had a way of making it seem like it made sense. She did, of course, emphasize that they would be helping her grandmother, and, after all, helping people always seemed like a positive thing. Still, something deep inside was warning him to tell the girl to get lost, to have nothing to do with her or her foolish ideas and head for the hills, instead he stayed, he listened, and he was convinced – that the practical joke would be fun for everyone involved. The girl promised no one would get hurt and that after it was all over he could go on about his day.

And so he found himself sneaking around the back of the old woman's house. Silently he crept through a window the girl said was always unlocked. Since there was no one around to worry about, he didn't find that odd: no one locked their windows or doors out this far in the woods. He made his way into the old woman's wardrobe and dressed in her nightgown and tucked himself into her bed. Even though the whole thing seemed very awkward, he let out a quiet chuckle. He could imagine how silly he looked and was thankful no other wolves were around to see him.

Not long after, the little girl in the red hood came into the bedroom on cue. They had previously rehearsed a short dialogue that she assured the wolf would greatly amuse her grandmother. The wolf was led to believe that her grandmother upon hearing the little girl enter the house, would come out from her knitting room to witness their interaction and feel thoroughly entertained, so the wolf did as instructed. The words only recently spoken echoed back to him.

"My, what big ears you have grandmother!" the girl said.

"All the better to hear you with." The wolf replied, sticking to the script.

"My, what big eyes you have grandmother!"

"All the better to see you with."

"My, what a big nose you have grandmother!"

"All the better to smell the basket of treats you brought me, dear sweet child."

In retrospect the wolf thought that he overdid it a bit, adlibbing the "dear sweet child" line. But it seemed to hit its mark with the girl who continued, "My, what big teeth you have grandmother!"

At this point the wolf was to scream "All the better to eat you with!" and then leap from the bed to chase the girl around the room. Looking back, this idea seemed like the worst one in the history of bad ideas, but at the time he was persuaded it would be the punch line that would have the old woman rolling on the floor. However, just as he uttered the line and threw back the bed covers, he heard a noise coming from the closet. The hooded girl had run to the closet and opened the door from which a bloody corpse collapsed onto the floor. The girl screamed so shrilly it pained the wolf's ears. Immediately a woodsman who just happened to be passing by stormed into the place gripping an axe.

And thus the accusations began flying toward the wolf. The girl explained to the woodsman that the she had just come in to visit her grandmother and believed the wolf to be her. She then denied ever seeing him before. She went on to blame the wolf for first killing her grandmother and then hatching a plan to trap and kill her as well. The wolf now knew that he had been set up. For some reason the girl knew about her grandmother's demise. For all the wolf knew she was responsible. But why? And why the elaborate ruse to blame someone else?

The woodsman raised his axe and went after the wolf, but the girl stopped him. She implored him to kill the beast outside not because she was afraid to see the violent act but because she was worried about making another mess in the bedroom. Reality then hit the wolf heavily. He figured the girl was getting the grandmother's place. He assumed she had concocted the whole scheme to get whatever was coming to her in the will. He knew there was no way the woodsman would take his word over the girl's and thought possibly they were in cahoots. That being the case, he knew he was in for it, and his hackles raised in anticipation of a battle.

Before another action could take place between him and the huntsman, the girl dropped to her knees. "No!" she screamed out. "No! I can't do it. I just can't!" The huntsman looked at her with great confusion on his face.

"What do you mean?"

She began sobbing hysterically but managed to speak between her tears. "I can no longer go through with this charade. The guilt has risen too much within me. I can no longer bear it."

"I think I can help you figure it out huntsman," the wolf interjected. See the kid here was more than likely in line to get this house from her grandma. For some reason, she didn't want to wait so she offed the old broad and tried to pin it on me."

"She didn't deserve this house!" the girl screamed, her guilt now turning to rage. "She was a greedy old woman who didn't care about her own son. That's right! She threw her own son out of the house and wrote him out of the will for having me out of wed-lock. That's right. I did kill her. I did want this house, but not now. Not this way. I don't know what happened to me. Something building up for so many years... It was just too much. Too much." She began to sob even more as the wolf and huntsman both went over to help her to her feet. As they were pulling her up off the floor, she turned to the wolf. "It was your eyes." she whispered. "Once I saw those beautiful eyes fill with fear I just couldn't... I just couldn't."

And at that moment the girl passed out. The emotional trauma had been too much for her. The authorities came and took her away. The wolf went about his business but would never forget that day. He would never again trust humans, as his opinion of them was forever changed by the girl in the red hood.

Genie in a Bottle

by Bryan and Wendy Schardein

Alex Dennison strutted down the trash-riddled street, one hand in his pocket and one holding a long stick, which he used to tap a rhythm on fences and walls. The afternoon sun made Brooklyn oppressively hot. Air conditioners hummed in windows, and children played in the spray of a fire hydrant. Alex whacked one of them across the ass with his stick as he passed.

"Ow!" the kid howled.

"What'd you say to me, punk?" Alex snarled, brandishing the stick like a baseball bat.

The boy, ten or twelve years old and so skinny his ribs were showing, raised an arm to ward off the blow. "Sorry, sorry!" he cried.

Alex made as if he were going to hit him, and the boy whimpered. "Remember who you're dealing with, kid." He turned away but stopped and whipped the stick around, catching the boy across the back and leaving an angry welt. "Don't let me see you around here again," he warned before starting back up the street.

He stopped into Manelli's Pizza to collect his normal fee and then proceeded down the street to Hamed's Antiques, where he found Old Man Hamed standing behind the counter. The guy had to be a hundred years old. His skin had darkened and wrinkled with age, and his face looked like a squishy prune. His eyes were clear and sharp, though, and he glared hatefully at Alex.

"Time to pay your weekly neighborhood association fees," Alex quipped as he stepped around the counter and roughly pushed Hamed away from the register.

"Please, this store is all I have. I can barely afford to live as it is."

Alex loomed over the shopkeeper. "I can make it so you don't have to worry about that anymore... or any other problems, for that matter."

Hamed held up his hands in surrender and backed away.

"Good. The neighborhood association would hate to lose such a distinguished member." Alex emptied the large bills from the register and stuffed them into his pocket; then he looked up to see Hamed holding a bottle. It was a kind of decorative decanter made of milk glass with golden stripes painted on it. On closer look, it appeared to be real gold embossed over the glass. It was bulbous at the bottom and narrowed near the top, where an ornate stopper with gold swirls rested.

"Hey, what's in that? Whiskey? I thought you types didn't drink."

"This is not for you," the old man said flatly.

"I think it is. Give it. Little something extra as a 'thank you' for my generosity." He yanked the bottle from Hamed's hands, then turned toward the exit. "Thank you for your support," he said over his shoulder as he sauntered out the door.

Alex strolled through the streets to the old brownstone where he lived with his mother, running up the stairs two at a time and slamming the door behind him.

"Don't slam the door!" Ma shouted from the kitchen.

"Shut up, Ma!"

"Watch your mouth! You're not too old for me to whoop."

"Yeah, whatever. Make me a sandwich."

"Make your own damn sandwich. You're eighteen years old and can take care of yourself. I'm going out."

"You're wearing too much makeup. You look like a whore."

Ma slapped the back of his head. "Don't talk to your mother like that! And don't wait up."

"Never do."

She left the apartment, slamming the door as she went.

"Yeah, she can slam it. Hypocrite." He made a ham sandwich and poured a pile of chips on the plate, then set his food on the table and held up the bottle. "Cheers," he said as he uncorked it.

With a whoosh, a cloud of blue smoke wafted out of the bottle and swirled in the air before him.

"The fuck?" Alex stood frozen in bewilderment as it took shape, coalescing into the form of a human.

"Human?" the figure before him spat as if it had read Alex's mind. It looked human, except for the fact that it was hovering four feet off the ground. It was a guy, Middle Eastern by the look of him, wearing loose, purple pants, vest, and shoes that were curled at the toes. His head was covered with a purple and gold turban adorned with a huge ruby. "I'll not be insulted in such a manner!"

"No way! That old man had a genie and he didn't use it to get rich? Stupid old guy. Or am I seeing things? Maybe I already drank whatever was in the bottle and it had LSD in it. Are you real? If you are, that means I get wishes, right?"

"It is in my power to grant you three wishes."

"Okay, I want – wait. Aren't you supposed to tell me something like, 'Be careful what you wish for'?"

The genie nodded. "All wishes come with a price."

"Yeah, but there's ways around everything, right? I wish for lots of money."

The genie nodded again. "Wish granted."

"There's this girl who lives around the corner. Felicia. I'd really like to see what's under that tight little skirt of hers. I wish to have sex with Felicia."

"Wish granted."

"And I want – wait, do I have to tell you right now?"

"You may ask your wishes at your leisure."

"I'll hold onto the third one, then. It may come in handy later; you know what I'm saying? So get back in the bottle now. That wasn't a wish."

"Understood." The genie swirled into mist and disappeared into the bottle.

"Damn it," Alex muttered. "Now I don't have anything to drink. I wish – ah-ha! Not gonna get me that easy!" He put his sandwich in the fridge and left the apartment, heading for the liquor store.

He stopped at the corner to wait for a car to pass, and a piece of paper, caught by the wind, hit him in the face. He reached up and took the paper away, then noticed it was a lottery ticket. "It can't be this easy," he laughed. "I gotta be already drunk."

At the liquor store, he handed the ticket to the cashier, a fiftyish woman with a blond bottle job. "Hey, is this worth anything?"

Her eyes widened as she scanned the ticket. She scanned it again and looked up at him with a broad smile. "This is your lucky day, sonny!"

"What? It's a winner?"

She turned the display on the scanner toward him, and he almost dropped the bottle of wine he had chosen. It was a winner all right – two hundred million dollars!

"Whoo!" Alex shouted, then leaned over the counter and kissed the older woman. "You know what? I'm gonna put this wine back. I'm goin' for a bottle of Cristal!"

***

Alex got his expensive champagne, and a Ferrari, and a fancy flat on Park Avenue, and a new set of friends. Well, he couldn't really call them friends, but he was still one of them, going to the best parties, drinking the finest wines, eating caviar. It tasted like shit, but who cared? He had found a great investment advisor and put a big chunk of his money into a company that couldn't lose. As much cash as he had now, lots more was coming his way. Life was sweet.

It wasn't all glitz and glamor, though. People from the old neighborhood called on him a lot, looking for a handout. His ma called him every day to bitch and whine about her living conditions, trying to make him feel guilty for not giving her any money. Hey, it wasn't his fault she hadn't played the lottery. And then there were the charities. Give us money for this. Donate money for that. He had worked hard for his money, and everybody wanted him to give it away! Forget it. They could go leech off somebody else.

Alex still liked to visit his neighborhood now and then, for no other reason than to flaunt his wealth. The first time he had done it, a kid had thrown a tomato at his car, and he'd beaten the little fart senseless and then made him wash the car. These days, the kids smiled and waved as he drove by, too scared to try anything like that again.

He pulled to a stop at the intersection and noticed Felicia standing at the corner, eying his Ferrari lustfully. Her deep-red hair cascaded over one shoulder. She wore a black spaghetti-strap top that was tight enough to show the pattern of lace on her bra through the thin material, and just short enough to give a glimpse of her toned midriff. Form-fitting jeans and high-heel sandals completed the outfit and reminded Alex of why he'd thought of her when he had made his wishes.

He rolled down the tinted passenger window, and Felicia started over. The sway of her hips and the slight jiggle of her breasts caused Alex's breath to hitch in his throat, and it took him a second to regain his composure. In that second, Felicia caught sight of him behind the wheel, and her face lit up as she leaned into the window.

"Alex, is that you? Oh, my God! Where did you steal this car? You are so going to get busted."

"It's mine, bought and paid for," he replied smugly. "Didn't you hear? I won the lottery. Wanna go for a ride and see how the better half lives?"

"Try and stop me," she dared, opening the door and sliding smoothly into the seat. She surprised him by throwing her arms around his neck and kissing him soundly on the cheek. "I always knew you'd make it big."

They tooled around the neighborhood for a while, and then Alex headed into Manhattan, where they stopped at a swanky restaurant downtown. He didn't even look at the name of the place; he just saw there were valets out front and pulled over. "One scratch and I'll make you wish you were never born," he warned as he handed over his keys.

"Of course, sir," the valet responded almost indifferently.

Inside, Alex fumbled through a hundred-dollar handshake with the maître d', and they were promptly seated. The meal consisted of small portions of overpriced froufrou, but it seemed to impress Felicia. He didn't even have to suggest going back to his place. She asked if she could see his apartment before they even finished the main course. Man, he thought, that genie really came through!

Back at his apartment, he poured wine, started the tour with the view of the city from the balcony, and finished it with the king-size bed and Jacuzzi in his bedroom. Before he could even ask what she thought, she wrapped her arms around his neck, pulling him close and covering his lips with hers. He froze for a moment at the suddenness of her embrace, but he opened his mouth to her as soon as he felt her tongue probing his lips.

"So, do you have a girlfriend?" she asked as she pulled back and gazed enticingly into his eyes.

"Um, no," he replied awkwardly. "That position has yet to be filled."

"Well, since we're talking about positions and being filled..."

"Who says we're just talking?"

Sex with Felicia was amazing, if brief. He was too excited to last more than a few minutes. If she was disappointed, he couldn't tell. He wasn't even sure he really cared.

When he woke up and she was gone, he thought, ah, so much the better. Alex crawled out of bed and went to the fridge, where he pulled out a beer. What the hell, it was noon already anyway. He sat on his balcony, watching the city go by, and jumped when his front door opened.

"Alex!" Felicia sing-songed as she entered, dropping two suitcases on the floor.

"Damn it, you scared the hell outta me!" he said. "I thought you were gone."

"No, baby, I just went home to get a few things." She wrapped her arms around his neck and gave him a long, wet kiss.

"Felicia, what are you doing?"

She pulled away and picked up one of her suitcases, heading for the bedroom. "Be a dear and grab that other one for me, will you?" She walked into the bedroom and set the case down, then went to his closet and started rearranging it. "I can see I've got my work cut out for me. Alex, really, you're so sloppy."

"Felicia!" he shouted. "What the hell are you doing?"

"Making room."

"Oh, no! You can't move in here."

"Well, of course, I can. You said last night you didn't have a girlfriend. Oh, by the way, Bloomingdale's declined your credit card."

"What?"

"I thought I would do a little shopping while I was out, so I took your card. But they wouldn't take it. I guess they figured I wasn't you, huh?"

She flitted about the room, moving clothes and accessories from one closet to another and ignoring his half-hearted protests until Alex finally stepped in front of her and grabbed her by the shoulders. "Felicia, no! You're not moving in. It was just one night."

She stared at him blankly for a moment, and then her eyes filled with tears and she let out a pitiful wail. "Oh, my God! I knew it was too good to be true! You bastard, you were just using me!"

She pushed him away roughly and threw a pair of shoes at him, then started lobbing all the other stuff on the bed, sobbing the entire time. All Alex could do was hold his hands up to ward off the flying clothing. When she finished with the clothes, she went to his dresser, picked up a bottle of cologne, and hurled it at him. It caught him in the temple, and he snarled in pain.

"Goddamn it, Felicia, get ahold of yourself!"

She finally crumpled to the floor, keening and moaning as if her mother had just died. "What am I gonna do? You can't leave me. We just got started, and now you hate me. You hate me!"

Alex was dumbfounded. Who could have known that Felicia was psychotic? How was he going to get rid of her? He needed time to think, and he couldn't think with her sitting on the floor blubbering like that.

He knelt at her side. "It's okay, baby, it's okay. You can stay for now."

"No, you're just saying that to make me feel better!"

"Hey, I tell you what: I've got about a thousand bucks cash in my wallet. You get yourself cleaned up, and you can take the cash to buy yourself something nice."

Felicia sniffled and looked up at him with mascara-smudged eyes. "Really? You mean it?"

"Sure, baby. You just caught me off guard, that's all."

With that, her entire demeanor changed. She smiled broadly, wiped her eyes, and wrapped her arms around his neck. "I knew you loved me." She kissed him and got up to go redo her makeup.

"Jesus Christ," he muttered.

She left the apartment half an hour later, and Alex bolted the door and grabbed another beer. He wondered if he could get a locksmith over to change the locks before she got back. He doubted it would solve the problem, though. All he had wished for was to sleep with her. Well, he'd certainly gotten his wish, but it was over now, and that should be that. He supposed he could just put his foot down and kick her to the curb, but she scared the hell out of him.

Hmm, maybe a hitman...

There was a knock on the door, and he opened it to find two men wearing dark suits. One had a thick manila folder tucked under his arm. "You're either the mob or the feds. I can't think of what either would want from me, so I think you've got the wrong address."

"Are you Alexander Dennison?" the taller of the two asked.

"Who's askin'?"

"Mr. Dennison, my name is Special Agent Barber, and this is my partner, Special Agent Allen; we're with the FBI. We have a few questions we'd like to ask you; may we come in?"

"You got a warrant?"

"No, Mr. Dennison. We aren't here to arrest you or search for anything; we just want to speak with you for a few minutes. We can do it out here, but we'd all probably be more comfortable sitting down, don't you think?"

Alex had the sudden, irrational fear that winning the lottery by genie was against some federal law, but he said, "Sure, whatever," and stepped aside for the men to enter. He led them to the living room, and they all sat down.

"Mr. Dennison, are you familiar with a company called Sahara's Odds?" Agent Barber asked.

"Sure. It's the company my financial advisor, Russell Tanner, had me invest in... some off-track betting place or something."

"Invest in?" Agent Allen echoed incredulously. "Mr. Dennison, we have documentation identifying you as president, CEO, and controlling shareholder. You know, when most people set up a Ponzi scheme these days, they try to make the company seem at least remotely legitimate. Sahara's Odds has no physical address, only a post office box – by itself not so unusual, but there's no record of the company owning any property at all. No business office, no equipment, nothing but the PO box and a cellphone number. It's miraculous that a company with so little foundation can 'guarantee' thirty-percent annual returns to its investors."

Alex had no clue what these two were talking about. His voice cracked as he sputtered, "Seriously guys, my, uh, financial advisor just told me he had this sure-thing investment that was gonna double my money. I don't know nothin' about being president or CEO or nothin'."

"Is this your signature?" Barber asked, pulling a sheet of paper from the manila folder and handing it to him.

Alex had signed so many things for Russell that he couldn't remember half of them, and he hadn't understood the legalese, anyway; but it did look like his signature. "I'm not sure."

The agent placed the paper back in the folder and stood up. "That's all we need at this time, Mr. Dennison. I must inform you, however, that the FTC is investigating your involvement in this as consumer fraud, the SEC is investigating separately for securities fraud, and the U.S. Attorney may open a third investigation. The assets of Sahara's Odds, and your own personal assets, have been frozen pending the outcome of these investigations."

"What does that mean?"

"It means you won't be able to use any of your lottery winnings for a while. I don't think I need to add, but don't leave town. We can show ourselves out." The agents left the apartment, closing the door behind them.

Alex's head was spinning. He didn't know what was going on, but he was going to find out, and Russell Tanner had better hope he was legitimate. Nobody messed with him like this. He dialed Russell's number, but the call went to an automated message saying the recipient's voicemail was full. Evidently Alex wasn't the only one trying, and failing, to get ahold of the guy. Alex knew without even talking to him that he was screwed.

"Goddammit!" he snarled as he threw the phone across the room. It crashed into the mantel and shattered. "Figures," he muttered, and went over to pick up the pieces.

As he stood by the fireplace with his broken phone, the genie's bottle fell off the mantel and landed in his hand, as if it were trying to get his attention.

"Oh, like I'm going to make a third wish now." No, there would be no more wishes. He was going back to that shop and smashing the bottle over Old Man Hamed's head. He'd thrash the guy for even giving it to him in the first place. He took the bottle and left the apartment.

It started to rain just as Alex got to the old neighborhood, and he couldn't find a parking space anywhere near Hamed's. His thousand-dollar suit was going to be ruined. As if that wasn't enough, when he reached Hamed's, he found the store closed.

Alex leaned against the door in the pouring rain, close to tears, and stared at the bottle, his reflection distorted in the curved gold plate. Why was all this happening to him? The genie had told him his wishes had a price. Who had known the price would be more trouble than the money was worth? If he ever got ahold of his so-called investment advisor, he'd ring his neck. Yeah, if he ever came back from sipping mai tais in Tahiti.

And what about the gold-digging psycho bitch? She was supposed to leave when he was done with her, but Alex had a feeling he wasn't going to get rid of her for a very long time.

He plodded back down the street and got into his car, where he placed the bottle in the passenger seat. "I just wish all of that would go away," he sighed, resting his head on the steering wheel.

"Wish granted," came the soft voice.

"No, wait, that wasn't a wish."

A sudden knock on his window made him startle, and he looked up to see a gun pointed at him. "Open the door!" the gunman shouted.

"You must be out of your mind, man!"

"Open it, or I'll smash the window." Alex didn't move, and the gunman used the butt of the pistol to break the window, covering Alex in glass; then he grabbed hold of Alex's collar with one hand and his hair with the other, and dragged him out through the window. The guy was incredibly strong, and when Alex's leg got caught on the steering wheel, he just yanked harder. The steering wheel didn't give, but his leg did. With a great crack, the leg broke, and the gunman managed to drag him the rest of the way out of the car. He tossed the screaming Alex unceremoniously onto the pavement, where he landed head first.

A blinding pain shot through his head, and the world began to swim. He was vaguely aware of the bottle, which his assailant tossed into the pool of blood that was rapidly growing next to his head.

The carjacker started the Ferrari and jerked it out into traffic, driving over Alex's pelvis in the process. Alex shrieked, but there was nobody around. He was alone, broken, and bleeding to death on a Brooklyn street with no one to hear his cries.

As darkness started to overcome him, he managed one last weak chuckle. Well, he had wished for it all to go away. It looked as though he had gotten his wish.

***

As Alex perished, the bottle began to wobble back and forth, and it finally tipped over and started rolling. It rolled down the street, through puddles and across potholes until it came to a ramp to the sidewalk. It rolled up the curb and continued on, finally stopping at the door to Hamed's Antiques. The door opened, and Hamed bent down and picked up the bottle.

"Ah, there you are, my friend," he said, locking the door behind him. He took the bottle to the counter and set it down, smiling as he watched the blue smoke filtering into the room. By the time the genie had fully materialized, the bottle was gone. The genie bowed his head and said, "It is done, Master. Your enemy is dead. Wish granted."

With that, he dissipated into smoke and retreated into his real home, a golden lamp which held a place of honor behind Hamed's counter.

Free to be Donnie Kinnaird

by Michael Williams

One look at Donnie Kinnaird told you someone had pissed in the gene pool.

I'm no looker myself, but my career started in the seventies when voices mattered more than looks, and even though I never had a big hit, I did all right, and here I was on American Superstar, offering advice to the hopefuls and wanna-bes, because they needed a country singer on the panel. I was sitting up at the table with that pretty little black singer Charisma Holmes and of course Nigel Carter, who was pretty much the son-of-a-bitch people made him out to be and thereby the most authentic man in the house.

Donnie was the image of the fattest boy in junior high, the fellow you picked on in my day, back before they called it "middle school" and before they called fat boys "about normal." He was dark-haired – some desperate shade of brown – and eyes both beady and loser-sullen. We came to find out he was monkey-clever, but the first impression is all looks, especially these days, and especially in this business.

And looks he did not have. He was the kind of boy you don't want on stage, but there he was.

So as his audition began, Donnie Kinnaird blinked in the light, and Nigel leaned forward in his chair and took a sip from a Pepsi I knew was spiked because mine was, too. Nigel was fixing to strap

---

* "At Seventeen" by Janis Ian
* "All Apologies" by Nirvana

the deer to the hood, and then this voice came out of the boy – that Radiohead song about the creep, the weirdo – and we all shut up, and halfway through the audition I look over and Charisma was in tears, but the boy was too damn ugly to be a star these days and we all knew it. Still, sometimes you let a drab little monster go through to L.A. and the auditions and you find a reason he can't cut it that isn't you're butt-ugly. That way you preserve the idea that anyone – yes, anyone, not just pretty people – can be a star, because this is America, goddamn it, the land of dreams.

So Charisma said yes, and Nigel said no because "the style is old-fashioned" and Charisma was all over Nigel for that – you know those manufactured arguments the two of them have every audition season. So the Guest Judge has to decide, which is me this year. And I'm thinking how sad it is to pass Donnie on to the next round, when he's dead in the water. But it might be his one chance to see L.A., I figured, which every young man should do, so I waved him through, and I sang his praises a little more than I should since I figured his big letdown was only a week or two away. I did it to irritate Nigel, who mouthed wanker at me, and Charisma gasped, but I only laughed because I didn't speak Brit. But Charisma and I hit it off from that point on. She thought I was tuned to some kind of artistry, I suppose. Truth was that anyone over thirty (which she was not) and cleansed of idealism (which she was not, either, being raised in the church, as sweet as Whitney before Bobby Brown and cocaine) knew that this was just televised karaoke, all about money.

Charisma took Donnie Kinnaird under her wing when we left for L.A., because you could tell that he was intimidated by the competition. He was one of ten contestants, what Nigel smugly called "a parade of archetypes," thinking Charisma and I didn't know what that was. There was Ramon Gutierrez, who had a four-octave range and girls screaming for him onstage, and then there was hip-hop Trevonte Carson, whose real name was Trevor and who was really in his last year at a New England prep school. There was Travis Troy Truitt, whose big hat and Southern accent hid the fact that he was really from Seattle. The main contenders among the girls were Waylene Meeks, a pretty blonde country singer from Alabama, and Bekki Tambo, who had come off one of those multi-racial Disney musical shows for pre-schoolers that sets out to prove the point that regardless of race, color, and creed, we all love a good, harmless, unbearably cute song. Those two wore long sleeve shirts: you'll find out why later. There was also Miranda – "just Miranda," as she told the press – letting drop the fact that her daddy was this famous movie star but that she wanted to make it on her own.

I knew how they felt. I hide that I read books and voted twice for Obama. Not that some of my fans don't do the same, but they all like their country stars archetypal, made to order.

There were others left in the competition – a couple of others whose names escape me. Every last one of them could sing some, enough to win a school talent contest (Ramon was different, a bona fide, and we were all hoping being Hispanic wouldn't be held against him by the voters) but Donnie was better than any of them. Except every single one of them was lovely, while Donnie was just himself, dumpy Donnie Kinnaird.

I liked that about him, though. John Lennon used to say, "Everybody's got somethin' to hide, 'cept for me and my monkey," but it seemed like Donnie Kinnaird was an exception to the rule – an authentic, gifted fatboy in a flock of gorgeous masquerades.

On the plane to L.A., Charisma sat beside Donnie and encouraged him. Girl was brilliant, I must allow, majoring on being yourself no matter what, never bringing up weight or looks but giving him all that positive, church-girl support and sitting back in economy class to be with him. I was back there, too, because country singers have the common touch. And it set a good contrast with Nigel, whose private jet was supposed to touch down a couple hours after we landed.

I listened in, and discovered Charisma had been pep-talking Donnie before. Had even given him things to read: "The Ugly Duckling" and Free to be You and Me.

Of course he was balking, for the usual reasons. He hated to read in the first place, and these books were for kids or old people. I couldn't blame him much. Free to Be was an old hippie text that told you how good you were no matter who you were, and "The Ugly Duckling" was another kind of fairy tale: Disney had done a movie of it, as I remembered.

Charisma was hard to argue with, all beautiful and with moist, heart-breaking eyes a teenaged boy could dream on. So Donnie had read what she had told him, and he had exhausting questions. Free to Be, he got: it was the kind of thing teachers lent out. But "The Ugly Duckling"? Was she trying to tell him something?

And of course she had to say no, no...that she wanted him to understand that the impression you make in your youth is superficial. That you grow and develop, like a thing of nature, and you find your community friends, who accept you not in spite of who you are but because of who you are.

But Donnie was monkey-clever, like I said before. And he had an angle on what he read.

"This ugly duckling thing," he said. "It's not just a story, is it?"

"How do you mean, baby?" Charisma asked, that sweet conversational voice almost singing above the rumble of the aircraft.

Donnie went on about how birds are misplaced in nature sometimes. He had Googled it, how they grow up in the wrong nests, and their foster parents never seem to know. And Charisma said, maybe so, baby, wish I'd finished college so I knew, and Donnie laughed and replied, Mother Nature's a bitch, isn't she, and Charisma gave a polite mmhmm. In a few minutes she got free and plopped down in the seat beside me, whispering, Lord amighty, that boy wears me out.

Gets on your last nerve? I asked her, but that wasn't how she meant it. He was polite enough. She claimed that his presence made her tired. Some misplaced energy about him. She needed a nap and retreated to her reserved seat in First Class, while I watched the last of the Star Wars films, the one where the pretty guy becomes Darth Vader. I was thinking that it figured when Skywalker got ugly he would get evil as well, and then Donnie Kinnaird sat down by me.

It was all Mister Anderson, this and that, and yes sir, but Charisma was right: there was something downright wearying about the boy, and I fazed in and out of the movie as he went on about the life of birds, stopping only when I made it pretty clear I was only listening out of politeness. He smiled, went back to his seat, and I just wanted to nap.

He left behind this smell. Not the Doritos-and-body-odor funk of fat boys his age, but a kind of astringent whiff that settled on the seat beside me, that made me tumble through drowsiness into a restless sleep, like I had been drugged or drained by his passage.

Or maybe it was because the flight was a redeye from Houston, and we arrived early in the Los Angeles morning and hit the hotel, where I lay face-down on an unturned bed for an hour, like I did on tour back in the '80s when I was really drinking – I mean dead serious about the bottle. It was fitful sleep, just like it was way back then, and I barely got to the auditorium by 10 when they were doing sound checks and some of the singers were already rehearsing back stage. Heard then that Trevonte Carson was sick – food poisoning from the redeye, they said, and there was talk of lawsuits because it sure didn't look like he would be up for singing that night.

None of the contestants was all that worried about it, seeing as it made for one less competitor, and by the time Nigel arrived in mid-afternoon, rested and ready, they had written off Trevonte for the evening, which meant that he was out of the competition. Of all the kids, only Bekki Tambo even pretended to mourn, and Travis Troy Truitt made some lousy crack about how it was strange that "a brother" would fall victim to bad barbecue, a remark that everyone shrugged off because they thought he was just Southern redneck white trash, and not a Seattle banker's son and a mean-spirited little dick.

Meanwhile, Donnie Kinnaird paddled above or around the drama. He retired to a side room off the stage and rehearsed with an accompanist – that old-school Janis Ian song – and you could hear that unearthly, misplaced voice rising from behind the closed door:

To those of us who knew the pain,
Of valentines that never came.
And those whose names were never called,
When choosing sides for basketball.

It was enough to break your heart, except by now I suspected he was milking ugliness for all it was worth.

Of course, Nigel worked Donnie over in the first round. Talked about how promising his audition had been, how we'd had such hopes, when all the while you could read the subtitles saying get off the stage you baboon, you've had your fifteen minutes of fame, now fuck off. But there was no elimination the first night because Trevonte's illness had seen to that. The kid was on a plane back to New Hampshire, done in by bad pulled pork and poetic justice, which meant that everyone who survived the airline supper survived to the second week. The Superstars all settled into rehearsal, and I settled into a cushy L.A. hotel room complete with open bar. I had the occasional light beer and watched baseball on cable, while Charisma hung with friends from her old girl group days and Nigel hauled in hookers to his third home up in Holmby Hills. Hiatus does that to entertainers: a long stay anywhere (and for us, that's over a week) throws you back into the person you really are when all is said and done.

Meanwhile, rehearsals continued, and the next two weeks took out the nameless kids who'd been added just to swell the numbers. Even so, Nigel tried throwing Donnie under the bus each week. By now he had his heart set on Bekki Tambo or Ramon Gutierrez, with no idea of the publicity risks they were hiding.

It was survival of the fittest. Darwin and the voting public took out what Nigel had failed to do. Those first two kids sang "I Will Always Love You" so that their versions washed up against each other and washed them out of the competition. Meanwhile, Donnie Kinnaird hibernated through rehearsal days – six hours or so with an accompanist, then coming out to sing tear-jerking lonely boy songs, Nirvana's "All Apologies" with a sly glance at Ramon, then gliding beautifully into the second verse,

I wish I was like you,
Easily amused
Find my nest of salt
Everything's my fault

The next week he returned to this rising version of "Creep" even better than his audition, bringing tears to my jaded eyes and to Nigel's, too, although the sumbitch recovered enough to blast Donnie for repeating a song until Waylene Meeks came on and sang the Dolly Parton version of "I Will Always Love You" and almost fouled her own nest. But Nigel, taken with her looks and image, said it was a "brilliant, original version that totally destroyed the others we heard before." It was clear he'd never heard Dolly's version, and Waylene became his favorite while we whittled the contestants down to seven.

Then you could only call a war of attrition. All the good will the kids showed on the flight to California vanishing as the stakes rose, Bekki not speaking to Waylene and Ramon taking a swing at Travis Troy, Miranda calling her father five to six times a day. Nigel called it "red in tooth and claw," but through it all Donnie, serene and hidden, expecting some kind of change.

By now, the ratings were at their highest of the season, and the votes were coming in through mobiles and laptops and the occasional land line. We were told that the lines went crazy when Bekki Tambo, high on the heroin she'd hidden for weeks, gave a groggy performance of Leonard Cohen's "Hallelujah" that ended mid-second chorus, when she nodded off on her feet and the auditorium sank into that kind of stunned silence that always comes when a career ends in public. Nigel joked later that it was "the addled girl disposing hallelujahs," but he wasn't laughing when she was next to go. Nursing a tall scotch and drawing on one of his menthols in the non-smoking hotel lobby, he confided to me that disaster seemed to follow this year's competition, and that at least it couldn't get worse, except that it always could. And as Bekki Tambo packed up to go back to one of those rectangular plains states, the next wave of chaos hit.

Travis Troy Truitt outed Ramon Gutierrez.

It all came from our Seattle cowboy's hearing Ramon exchanging endearments in a tearful phone call with someone named Dimitri back in Miami. Ramon had been the clear front-runner, and the boys had clashed on several occasions, the last one, of course, when Ramon had kicked Travis' ass and "T-cube," as Charisma had called him scornfully (because by now we all hated him) had staggered onto stage, his shiner still lavender under a layer of funeral-home-thick makeup, and completely made horseshit of a Garth Brooks song that was halfway to horseshit before he took it on. His lot had been imperiled that week, and if it hadn't been for Bekki Tambo's disaster he might have been the next to go.

Then again, Donnie Kinnaird hadn't gotten any prettier, so you could never be sure who'd have been next. But the outing marked the end of Ramon Gutierrez, because Americans don't like gay people, and of Travis Troy Truitt as well, because nobody likes a tattletale.

So the last week – the final of American Superstar – came down to Waylene Meeks, Miranda, and Donnie Kinnaird. Boy versus girls, country versus pop versus emo, South versus everywhere else – it was all masquerade for pretty versus ugly, so barring a disaster, we knew who wasn't going to win. And yet in that last week of preparations, there was a gloom over the whole competition.

One night, before I left the studios for the hotel, I was walking down one of the corridors, and there was Waylene, seated on the floor, hugging herself, her back against the wall. I stood over her, then crouched, all the while asking honey what's wrong? what's wrong? and thinking, sweet Jesus the last thing we need is another junkie.

She looked up, and her eyes were clear. But tired, way tired.

"Nothing, Mr. Anderson," she said. "It's just the stress of this contest. I have things in me that need to come out, that I was born to express and show. Sometimes I'm afraid I'm too weary to go on stage, but I guess that's when you remember your raising, ain't it? Where you draw on what Mamma and Daddy taught you."

It was a perfect country contestant speech, like something she'd deliver onstage, and I didn't know whether it was faked or genuine, so I gave consolation, reassurance, not knowing if it was fake or genuine, either, just hoping that somewhere, after years of entertainment, it was tapping into my better nature.

Meanwhile, Nigel was trying to hook in some real celebrities for duets with the Final Three, but Pink and Christina and John Mayer turned him down flat out, and even Britney said there were some things too toxic.

When Courtney Love turned him down – the widow herself in an "All Apologies" duet with Donnie Kinnaird, which showed how desperate Nigel had become – he just said fuck it all, and billed the final week as Superstar Unplugged –"nothing between you and the stars but the voices." Everyone knew it was bullshit, but it was Nigel, so we nodded and faked enthusiasm.

The contestants were to sing their best song – the one they thought "reflected who they were," but it boiled down to the one they did the best, the big vote-getter. Their choices were predictable, but other things weren't, and the night before rehearsals Charisma and I sat down in her dressing room and compared bleak and anxious notes.

"To be honest," she said, "it's almost the devil's work."

I nodded politely, and it could have explained much, except Donnie Kinnaird was no devil. It was only months later that I understood, after he'd won the contest, when Charisma called me and told me to Google "brood parasitism."

You see, Donnie Kinnaird had been right all along about this ugly duckling business. That it does happen in nature. There are birds that lay their eggs in another bird's nest – a different kind of bird altogether, where the young are smaller, more frail, more vulnerable than the transplanted hatchling, young that will wither away while the parasite grows and prospers. The cuckoo and the cowbird, but there's also this South American duck that's notorious for it, so it's like the swan in the fairy tale, I suppose.

The original Ugly Duckling.

But we had no idea that night. Each of us rooted for Waylene Meeks. Because Miranda and Donnie both were, now that I think of it, misplaced birds.

The auditorium was filled, that strange, astringent smell in the air below the smell of sweat and a hint of weed, and you could tell from the hollering that Waylene was the favorite. Miranda's celebrity daddy was there, right behind Ramon and Travis Troy (who had been strong-armed into sitting together and acting like they had made up, because that's what we do in America, god damn it!), and just framing the three of them in a single camera shot was enough to conjure up a number of hatreds.

And Miranda's old man mouths love you, baby straight into the camera when Miranda's name is announced, throwing her under the bus for a photo opportunity. And she sang first, the camera cutting to his reactions as she did that Jennifer Hudson Dreamgirls song all monstrous and distorted, straining for trills as her little hand groped the air like she was trying to snatch a chance of winning, like the world's most desperate Beyonce impersonation, and the camera cutting to Daddy's frown because nobody likes desperate and, judging from the muted applause, nobody much liked Miranda.

Second to sing was Waylene, and as she launched into the old Dolly Parton number, I sat back and prayed she'd nail it, because Miranda was an entitled, impossible little bitch, and Donnie was the creep, the weirdo. This was Waylene's threshold to stardom, and if she won she would join a whole parade of beautiful blonde country girls who sounded alike and drew similar, seven-figure paychecks.

Waylene got to the second verse, the one about bittersweet memories, and opened her arms to embrace all of America, her white cotton blouse as down-home and simultaneously pure as a girl could muster, and I'm thinking she's perfect and Charisma's crying because she's thinking of poor dead Whitney who sang it, too. Nigel's at the end of the table, his eyes glazed and his face broken with that half-smile because he's counting the money, he's going to produce the record.

And then Waylene expresses what she's held inside. The pressure and the doubt and the sapping weariness, as the girl's arms blossom red on the white, the blood seeping through the cotton as the cuts she's been giving herself the past year open in front of twenty million people.

She went on singing for a spell, but the audience tumbled into silence, then the accompaniment. Waylene sang a bar or two a capella, then gets the point, looks at her blood-soaked shirt and lurches off-stage with a cry.

Cut to commercial, and a rush of directors and assistants. Nigel stays in his seat, and Charisma runs backstage to help out Waylene, because that's Charisma's thing, that's her rep. I take a long draw from the bourbon and Pepsi, then look onto the stage where they're preparing Donnie Kinnaird for "All Apologies".

Because you move on, people, you move on. In nature and the industry and in America.

And when the lights go up and Donnie slides into the first few bars, the crowd's back in their seats. And he sings it "for Waylene," he says softly, dripping sympathy and sweeping in the last undecided votes, and as the song reached its end he raises his hand, stilling the accompaniment, and gestures to the crowd as he sings the fade, beckoning them to sing along. Which they do, until the only voices in the auditorium not joining in are mine and Nigel's, and the two of us look at each other in horror, knowing full well where this would head from now on.

All around us the words of the Cobain boy. The one we all chewed up and spit out:

All in all is all we are
All in all is all we are

Red White and Corpse Blue

by Jason Walters

> "Children, children, let me live,
> Snowy-white, Rosy-red,
> Will you beat your lover dead?"
> —Grimm's Fairy Tales, Snow White and Rose Red

There was no denying it: Hank's Hualapai Club smelled like piss.

It smelled like a lot of other nasty things too. Stale beer. Last year's cigarettes. Old sweat. Dust. Half remembered dreams that had curled up and died thirty years before. Still, there was nowhere else to be on a Friday night in the town of Hualapai, Nevada if you wanted to enjoy the dubious company of your equally dubious fellow townspeople.

And it was warm. That was a big deal when the temperature outside hadn't been above sixteen degrees for the last month, propane had gotten so expensive that everyone was heating their double-wides by burning left over shipping pallets and sagebrush, and every pipe leading to every sink and every toilet in town had been frozen for almost the entire hellish time. That last part naturally led into the first: the toilets in the bar's hadn't worked in weeks. Everyone knew that. Yet everyone kept pissing in them all the same.

Maybe it was the alcohol. January was the month of alcohol.

Rose Red towered up behind the bar like some kind of tainted goddess, all scarlet curls, tits, contempt, and managerial skills.

Every man in town wanted to fuck her. But every one of them was too intimidated to try, no matter how many cans of Bud Light they guzzled or Irish Car Bombs they imbibed. They didn't joke about it. They didn't even try to put each other up to it. When Rose Red gave you that look – and she always gave you that look – you knew that if you whipped it out it was never, ever going back in. Even the way she cleaned glasses and pulled pints screamed "Castration!"

And she didn't like girls, either. Which just made her even more scary.

At a little past nine Rose's sister came in. She took her usual seat at the far end of the bar, holding court far away from the door, and began chain smoking over a cosmopolitan. Unlike her sister she was small and thin, with shoulder-length straight black hair and unblemished skin the color of milk. Also unlike her sister she was easy. Or so everyone said. Nobody had actually managed it – though everybody knew somebody who knew somebody who supposedly had. But she was definitely more friendly in a distant, slightly condescending manner that was in some ways harder on the male ego than her sister's more straightforward animosity.

This was the the typical nine to midnight scene for the two women; the large, frightening redhead glowering and threatening the men who swarmed around her tiny sister, who insulted them through a thick curtain of Virginia Slim smoke in various ways they were too unsophisticated or drunk to understand. It was like this night after night; a sad, comic tableau of the sort that fleshes out small town life, making it more interesting and thus more bearable.

Which made the fact that it all came to an end one frosty night all the more remarkable. It would be some time before any of the snow-dazed and nicotine-stained denizens of the club realized what had actually happened.

Or the law, for that matter.

***

Chaunte Harris was not a normal-looking black woman. But she wasn't a normal anything, so a natural blend of carrot-red hair, striking green eyes, and freckles on caramel brown skin framed by an extremely conservative and tasteful pinstriped business suit simply added to her mystique. Unlike most of

Washoe County's upper-level management, she conducted the majority of her business from a park bench in the front plaza of its main East 9th Street offices, comfortably ensconced in a protective fog of cigarette smoke while smartphones, netbooks, half-finished cups of Starbucks coffee, and subservient bureaucrats orbited around her like moons circling a rotund, yet oddly irresistible, planet. In the bitter winter months, she retreated into a nearly Ethiopian restaurant, replacing her trademark Parliament Light 100's with a Blu e-cigarette and her half-empty coffee cups with endless helpings wat-on-injera.

Harris worked this way for several reasons, the first of which was that she could. Twenty long, hard years climbing her way up the county bureaucracy had put her in a position that was unassailable from below by way of her seniority, and untouchable from above by way of her race – or at least the one of several potential racial choices she had been clever enough to use when applying for a county job. The second was that those same twenty years of mastering the finer points of a particular and peculiar western county's laws had slowly turned her into something of an anarchist, or at the very least a libertarian. She didn't actually like The Law as a concept, and she enjoyed snubbing her nose at the very system that was slowly, inexorably putting the money together to pay for her retirement. The visible sign of her distaste for the county's petty, pointless intrusions into the lives of its inhabitants was her distinctive method of conducting her daily business. The far-less visible one was her tendency to let the "small fish" go, so that she could focus her attention on those individuals and corporations which seemed to be actually guilty of doing something bad for the public health.

Finally, she didn't like a certain kind of personality that gravitated to low-level county inspection jobs. Petty. Arrogant. Particularly suited to excessing power over the defenseless. "Chickenshit," her grandfather would have called them. They were the bane of 21st Century American life, and there was a far better chance of avoiding such people on a day-to-day basis if one simply avoided the places where they liked to congregate. Like the cubical-strewn rooms of Washoe County's East 9th Street offices. Being even a few meters outside seemed to make it existentially more difficult for those sorts of people to find her, even though they knew precisely where she was. The context – or, perhaps, lack of context – unnerved them.

She sighed and blew out a long plume of water vapor as a particularly repulsive example of that species strode past the buffet table toward her. He was a small man with all that generally entails. His mousy brown hair was exactly the same length as his scraggly beard, which hung below a pinched face slightly resembling that of an angry terrier. It swiveled back-and-forth above the sort of of short sleeve and necktie combination that could never be popular, even in northern Nevada where temperatures rose regularly above 100-degrees in summer. He even wore them in winter. She wasn't sure she'd ever seen him smile. In fact, she wasn't certain she wished to.

"Good morning Levi. Is there something I can do for you?" In spite of her distaste for Levi Wells, he was one of her subordinates, and she owed him at least a basic sort of politeness.

"Yeah, Chaunte: send someone else 100 miles out to Hualapai. I hate that redneck, peckerwood trailer park of a town." There didn't seem to be anything Harris could to do convince Wells that she wasn't impressed by that kind of talk. She found "reverse" racism just as distasteful as the normal variety. Nor did he seem to grasp that she preferred to be called "Mrs. Harris" at work. So she'd given up on explaining both some years back, and simply accepted the limited little man for what he was: namely, a leg-humping nuisance.

"Someone has to go once a year Levi. Why not you?" She asked evenly. "Just go out there, pass the two or three businesses they have, and come back. There's nothing to it."

The small man scowled, showing off his yellow, perfectly spaced teeth.

"That place is so..." She could see him struggle for the right label, think of one, discard it, think of another, discard that, and finally shrug. " Well, white trash I guess. I mean: it's everything we're trying to move modern Nevada away from. It's not reactionary, exactly. I mean, they hold Burning Man there, right? But the state needs to have standards, you know? And we can't so long as there are still towns built out of 70's double-wides and cinder block buildings. Nobody should live there."

"So don't live there. You're not a building inspector. Just do your job and come home."

"It's a waste of a day." He complained. "We've got real people here in Reno that actually need our help and guidance."

"Look Levi," she leaned forward, a strained-but-sympathetic expression on her face. "Just go up there and do your job. Don't offer any opinions, don't go out of your way to find violations, and don't screw with the locals. Especially that last part. You might not like them, but they definitely won't like you, and they can smell contempt like a dog smells meat. So just head out there in the morning, and you'll be back in Reno doing..."

God, she thought. What does he do with his free time? It made her want to shiver.

"...well, whatever you do in no time. Okay?"

The small man nodded, not looking particularly convinced. She sighed, inwardly this time.

Oh, hell. This isn't going to go right for anybody.

***

Handsome Brown was, as his name implied, handsome. He looked a lot like Smokey And The Bandit-era Burt Reynolds, only a few shades darker. But he had the mustache, the smile, and the manly chest hairs. And the the girls. Girls liked him a lot. He was popular.

Handsome wasn't a complicated guy. He liked his job. He liked fishing two or three times a year in the 40-foot double-masted sailboat his brother kept in Cabo San Lucas. He drove the Schwans delivery route from Reno almost to the Oregon boarder twice a month. This would have made him popular even if he hadn't looked like a Spanish Burt Reynolds. Without Schwans its was practically impossible to get ice cream, frozen TV dinners, or pies in Hualapai.

After a long day of driving from farm to ranch to double-wide selling 12-dollar key lime pies, Handsome would often stop by Hanks for an equally overpriced Corona — and the chance to flirt with Snow White and Rose Red. It was an innocent, understated thing really. One of those comfortable dalliances adults have that never really amount to anything.

Until one day they do.

***

Uncle Hank had been out of town for weeks on the day Levi walked through the door of his bar, leaving the day-to-day running

of the place to Rose Red. Not that the health inspector had any
way of knowing that. Or that he would care very much if he did.
Given what Uncle Hank was doing at the exact moment Levi's
sensible brown loafers crossed his establishment's fetid threshold,
it's unlikely the old man would have cared very much either.

The first thing the little man noticed was the terrible smell.
That would have been enough – in fact was was most certainly
enough – to make him want to vomit. But it was the decor that
caused him to briefly shiver with horror and wrath. 1980's
Budweiser mirrors. Damaged floors. Out-of-date slot machines
that still took quarters. Out-of-date Right Wing bumper stickers.
"Collectible" whiskey bottles shaped like skeletons on motorcycles.
An ancient jukebox that played scratched recordings of David
Allen Coe songs. The sort of tiny, alcoholic island you used to find
on any street corner in Sparks, all now subsumed under a rising
tide of Panda Expresses, Whole Foods, and REIs. A refuge for
exactly the sort of people Levis Wells knew in his heart should
have no refuge.

Levis squared his shoulders and walked through the afternoon
cloud of cigarette smoke and overly loud Conway Twitty songs to
face the frightening Amazonian bitch who loomed over the scarred
alter of the bar. She eyed him with all of the warmth of a first year
medical student preparing to dissect a cadaver as he pushed his
way forward past a couple of 70-year-old cowboys in filthy dusters.

He pointed to the identification on a lanyard around his neck.

"County health inspector. May I speak with the owner of this
establishment?"

The big woman shook her head ponderously from side to side,
trying to figure out what to do. It really wasn't a good time for a
surprise health inspection. Besides the obvious stench and filth,
the soda gun was utterly filthy. So filthy in fact that the rubber
cup it rested in was covered in slime, and she suspected that the
hose inside was so crusted with God-knew-what that, could one see
it, it would look like an alien life form in an incubation phase. The
bottles were dusty, the sink was filled with dishes, and the counter
tops were sticky. Actually, everything in the place was sticky.

County health inspectors always came to Gerlach
unannounced, though typically the managers of its various
businesses warned one another the moment one was spotted,
setting off a cascade of furious bleaching and scrubbing. Hank's
must have been the first in line. Usually they checked the booze,

looked over the bottles to make certain they were clean, checked the bathrooms, inspected the ceiling for leaks, and made certain the ice cooler was empty. Typically Hank's would squeak by with the lowest possible ranking that still allowed it to stay open.

Not this time, she reflected. And then decided to balls it out with brutal honesty.

"Hank hits all of the but huts in Pahrump this time of the year. Is there something I can do for you?"

"Yes, actually." He wrinkled his nose in disgust. "May I ask what that smell is?

"Yeah: piss." She responded matter-a-factly, still set on toughing it out. "Most of the town's plumbing has been frozen for over a month, and our crappers don't work. It sucks, but you can't keep a drinking man from pissing. And if he goes outside at night it will probably freeze off. So what can you do?"

"What. Can. You. Do?" he responded blankly, his disbelief completely lost on the woman. "Well, I don't now what you can do madam, but I..."

It was right then that he saw her.

"I..."

It was like a scene in one of those MTV videos where the camera zooms in on an erotic tableau framed by overwhelming, colorful images. Only with cigarette smoke and flashing neon instead of rose peddles and Madonnas radiant with light.

"I..."

She was gliding toward him on a frictionless surface of perfection. OR maybe he was just walking toward her. It was hard to say. One way or the other he was beside her before he knew what he was doing.

"I..."

Red and White exchanged a glance, followed by a very subtle nod. She leaned into his body space rather than doing what most women did. Namely, instinctively move away.

"I what handsome?" Snow White purred. "Could it be 'I'd like to buy you a drink?' or 'I'd like to buy you a pack of cigarettes?'"

He bought her both. He even tipped Red.

***

Four hours later a drunken Levi Wells staggered out of Hank's, falling over the the crumbling lip of its cement porch as he went.

His limped to his car and drove off, his head filled with vague promises of evening pleasure.

The two sisters watched him go.

"Well, fuck." Said Rose Red.

Snow white blew a smoke ring.

"That's exactly what ain't gonng happen."

Her big sister snorted.

"You've done worse. Just do it and he'll go away."

The smaller woman shuttered.

"If I do it he'll never go away."

"But if you don't do it he'll shut the place down. I won't be able to pay our rent, and we'll end up living in the back room of mom's singlewide in Sun Valley. Again."

Snow White shuddered once more.

***

Levi sat in his car for hours, smelling himself and listening to the weird country-cum-rave station that was only broadcast around the town of Hualapai for reasons he couldn't fathom. It wasn't a very nice smell. But he really didn't have anywhere to go. He'd driven almost two blocks before realizing that he had no clear idea why he'd driven away at all. So he'd pulled over and left the car running, its heaters desperately struggling to ward off the freezing February winds outside.

He glanced at this watch. Shit. Still an hour left to go. Was it too much to ask a station not to back George Strait with the Chemical Brothers?

He hadn't realized how drunk he'd gotten until he began to sober up. It wasn't a nice feeling, or one that he was very familiar with. But he knew the only sure way to fix it was to drink more. Which he knew he would undoubtedly would.

In another... 47 minutes.

***

She couldn't stand his touch. And that's why she hit him the first time.

Things had gone as planned at first. The health inspector had returned right at closing time, coming in as the regulars were going out. Rose had locked the doors behind them and made herself scarce. Then the little man had come to her, hesitant at first, then insistent. In her body space. Expectant. Wanting. His erection pressed against the side of her leg as he stood next to her bar stool. His yellow, perfectly rectangular teeth leered at her.

She'd been drinking since he'd first left the bar. (Actually, she'd been drinking well before then, but that hadn't really felt like drinking, you know?) And she'd been serious about it, too, taking shot after shot of Jägermeister in an attempt to make the whole thing alright. But it wasn't alright. She'd simply drunk herself into an angry sober.

So she hadn't been acting consciously when she'd reached behind the counter, grabbed a bottle of Canadian Hunter, and shattered it over his head. He'd dropped like the sack of shit he was. Then she'd begun stomping him with her stiletto heels. Later she vaguely remembered beating him with a pool cue until it broke.

When Rose returned several hours later the little inspector was blue, his eyes bulging from the shattered head of his corpse as it lay sprawled across the floor before the bar stools, neon lights flickering across dead flesh. The tavern's battered, uneven floor was covered in blood. So was her sister, who sat weeping in the center of a gore-splattered pool table, her face in her hands as the jukebox banged out yet one more desperate version of "The Road Goes On Forever" by yet more more desperate outlaw country hack.

"Well. Fuck. Me." The big woman once again turned her head slowly from side to side, taking in the scene as she tried to figure out what to do. Finally she shook herself, quickly locking the front door of the bar behind her and striding over to her hysterical sister, her feet making soft squelching sounds as she went.

"Honey?" She shook her sister softly. The weeping woman didn't respond. So she shook her harder, at which point Snow White leaned over the side of the pool table and wretched, adding a new scent to the rich aromatic confluence of piss, cigarette smoke, and blood that impregnated the interior of Hank's Haulapai Club.

***

Rose Red was dragging the body out of the service entrance by its feet when she backed into Handsome Brown. The delivery man dropped the milk crate of ice cream he was carrying in surprise, but quickly recovered. Rose though that it probably wasn't the first corpse he'd ever seen.

"Friend of yours?" He asked surprisingly casually.

"Not really."

"Good. If he was, I'd hate to think of what you do to your enemies."

They both stood there for a moment just staring at each other. Then Handsome looked down at the body.

"I guess I'd better give you a hand with that," He said evenly, reaching down to grab the shoulders. "He'll fit nicely into the back of the truck."

She nodded.

"Does he have a car?" He continued. "We'd probably better take care of that too. There's a ravine about twenty miles up the road from here..."

***

The sun was well over the sea of Cortez when Handsome killed the engine and just let the boat drift, it's twin masts gently rocking back and forth far above. El Arco de Cabo San Lucas was clearly visible in the distance, a distinctive mouth of stone that shot out of tongues of white foam as the warm waves struck it. He sighed contentedly, then took another sip from his Paloma, enjoying the taste of tequila and grapefruit in his mouth. Then he walked skillfully along the starboard side of the boat, his hand clinging to the brass rail as he swung one foot over another along a Durabak-coated ledge.

Rose Red lay sprawled on an old blanket across the front deck. She wore a bikini whose russet red surface matched her hair, a Tecati clutched in one hand and a cigarette in another. The swimsuit left very little to the imagination.

"Roll over," said Handsome, lowering himself down onto the deck next to her. "I'll put some suntan lotion on your back."

"How about my front?" She teased, turning herself lazily over.

"Oh, we'll get to that later." He replied with a smile. She sighed contentedly as he began to rub Coppertone all over her body, kneading it into her back and shoulders with skillful fingers. "They'll be after us by now you know. They must have found him and his car down in that ravine."

"Yep," he replied, his hands working down toward her buttocks.

"You know, Mexico has an extradition treaty with the States." She continued, enjoying the feel of his large palms on her ass.

"Yep." He continued working his way down with the oil, massing it into the back of her legs.

"So what do you plan on doing about it?"

"Oh, I imagine Jesus will save us."

Feminine, high-pitched giggles came from the cabin below, followed by moans in a low, husky male voice, followed by yet more giggles. Rose Red rolled her eyes in mock indignation.

"My sister and your brother have been going at it for days now!"

"Well, now, not everybody can be as chaste as us," he replied with gravity. Rose sighed.

"Really, Handsome: does your brother ever work?"

"Well... Jesus is chief of police for all of Baja California Sur, and rank has its privileges. He is after all a very busy man. And, really, what are three more drunken gringos among the tens of thousands that there are down here at any given time? Very, very hard to find."

She giggled. It was a deeper, somehow more feminine sound than the startled squeaks her sister bleated out, he thought. He kissed the back of her neck. A moment later, she kissed him somewhere else.

There was no denying it: Cabo San Lucas smelled like sea air, suntan oil, and redhead.

About the Authors

L. Andrew Cooper's anthology entry "Kindertotenlieder" stems from the dark world developed in his horror novels *Burning the Middle Ground* (2012) and *Descending Lines* (2013). His non-fiction includes the books *Gothic Realities: The Impact of Horror Fiction on Modern Culture* (2010) and *Dario Argento* (2012) as well as the co-edited textbook *Monsters* (2012). A regular film critic for WDRB-TV, Andrew teaches film studies at the University of Louisville. His short stories and essays have appeared in *Blood Reign Literary Magazine*, *The Realm Beyond*, *Gothic Studies*, *Horror Studies*, *Slayage*, the forthcoming *Encyclopedia of the Zombie* (June 2014), and elsewhere. He believes smart people have imaginations and aren't afraid to follow them into the darkest corners in search of the brightest lights. Visit him at www.landrewcooper.com.

William Levy has always lived just past the fringe. Hailing from Kentucky, he has been a circus roadie, doughnut chef, hospital courier, weapons system designer, and Presidential Scholar in Physics. He's spent the last 35 years as a freelance illustrator, cartoonist, and game designer, in the last decade adding writer to the list. He currently resides in a comfortable bungalow in the magical kingdom of Louisville, with his talented sculptress bride and muse Karen. Their somewhat  empty nest, post three grown children, is filling up nicely with his lifetime collection of books, movies, and comics, guarded fiercely by two hybrid rhino tabbies and the world's smartest dog.

Christopher Kokoski is a professional author, trainer and speaker. His published credits include the novels *Dark Halo* and *The Past Lives series*, the nonfiction book *101 Ways To Pray Better and Get Faster Results,* the short stories *Drown* and *By the Hair of My Chinny-Chin-Chin*, national training materials, and dozens of articles, including one peer-reviewed journal article that he uses to impress people much smarter than himself. He is deeply grateful to God, his family and to the gift of  storytelling, which he naïvely believes can transform the world.

G.L. Giles had hundreds of signings at most major chain bookstores and many wonderful independent bookstores in the Southeast and Midwest over the last decade. She's been on television 10 times talking about her YA, adult and children's picture books—on various stations in South Carolina, Georgia, and Alabama—and in 2008 she was interviewed by the legendary Joe Franklin (on his Bloomberg Radio show). She's also not a stranger to YouTube at

this point with one of the videos on her books at over 73,000 views. In addition, Giles hosts interviews at her WordPress blog: The GL Giles Files. To add to that, Giles's "Water Vamps" (2nd ed.) hit #3 in YA Horror (in Amazon's 'Free in Kindle Store') in 2013. She also writes children's picture books ("Hurricane Hound" and "The Clever Cat That Could") as Gia Lee. Admittedly both feline and canine crazy, yet determined to break the 'crazy cat lady' stereotype, Giles lives with her handsome husband, seven cats, and one 'pittie' in rural South Carolina.

Georgia L. Jones is an author and entrepreneur. She resides in the beautiful Ozarks with Donny her husband, Michael her son, and Tank, a 3 year old English Mastiff. Her published works include, Legends of Darkness and Witches from the "Remnants of Life" (Urban Fantasy) series, 2012 Survivalist Handbook (Political Humor), and several anthology contributions. After owning Aphrodite's Hair & Nails for 15 years she sold it in 2013 to pursue other interests. She is currently enjoying working on several writing projects, getting another small business off the ground, restoring their 1840 home...and just enjoying life with her family!

Once upon a time in a valley not so far away, lived a young boy named Brad. He grew up with visions of comic books and cartoons in his head, which made his imagination grow and grow. He drew as much as he could until he became quite good at it. His creative visions would flow through many avenues leading him to write and play songs, create logos, write and draw comic strips and even make web sites, signs, and all manner of computer graphics. Eventually his imagination convinced him to write down a series of stories occurring in strange lands, and thus he began to explore the path of creative writing, some of which you see here today.

Bryan Schardein is a software engineer and chess coach for middle and high school students. He also teaches martial arts in his rare moments of free time. Wendy Schardein has recently fulfilled her dream of becoming a full-time author and artist. She is currently working on a set of tarot cards, which she hopes to have available late in 2014. Bryan and Wendy have published one novel together  and are currently working on a second. They have been married since 2005 and live in Louisville, Kentucky, in a big, loud, crowded, messy, happy house with Wendy's mother, three teenagers, two dogs, a ghost, a part-time sparrow, and a partridge in a pear tree.

Michael Williams has written a dozen novels and a number of short stories and poems. His most current books include *Vine* (2012) and *Trajan's Arch* (2010). He teaches at the University of Louisville and lives in Corydon, Indiana, with his wife, Rhonda, and too many cats.

Jason S. Walters is an author, essayist, and publisher best known for running Indie Press Revolution (IPR), a distributor of micro-published roleplaying games. He is also one of a small group of investors that purchased Hero Games in 2001, and serves as its CEO. After owning a San Francisco bike messenger service for 15 years, he and his wife Tina moved to Midian Ranch: a homestead near the town of Gerlach, Nevada. It is also the location of IPR's warehousing complex. They have a daughter with Down syndrome named Cassidy and animals too numerous to mention.

Also from BlackWyrm...

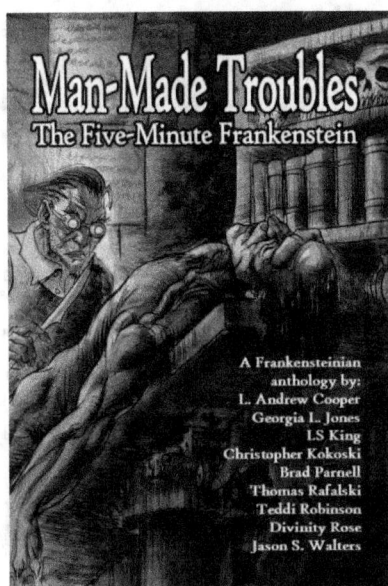

Man-Made Troubles
The Five-Minute Frankenstein

Today's most talented authors build upon the original themes and topics to present new ghastly fiction based on many of the various aspects of the original Frankenstein story. But there was a catch to the assignment – each story could only be four pages long. [Horror Short Stories, ages 14+]

Burning the Middle Ground

by L. Andrew Cooper

This dark fantasy about small-town America transforms fears about the country's direction into a haunting tale of religious conspiracy and supernatural mind control. Burning the Middle Ground has as much appeal for dedicated fans of fantasy and horror as for mainstream readers looking for an exciting ride. [Supernatural Horror, ages 18+]

THE OGRE
AND OTHER STORIES

by William Levy

Once Upon a Time, in the Forest of Masks and Dreams, there lived an Ancient Ogre…

When reality and fantasy become roommates, these fables of a lost soul in an improbable realm give a glimpse into aspects of life, touching us all.

[Pensive Fantasy, ages 18+]

DARK HALO

by Christopher Kokoski

A winged stranger appears during a violent lightning storm, chasing Landon Paddock out into the maddening night with his estranged 15-year old daughter.

As layer after layer of reality is dissolved by a series of violent encounters, the only way to survive might be for Landon to band together with the family he destroyed to make one last stand against a sinister army of unthinkable magnitude.

[Supernatural Horror, ages 14+]

WATER VAMPS
a young adult adventure story
by GL Giles

Take a both fun-filled and treacherous ride into the waters surrounding the peninsular city of Charleston, South Carolina with G.L. Giles's water vampires. Slake your thirst for different vampire species and subspecies at the same time!
[Young Adult Horror, ages 12+]

Remnants of Life: Legends of Darkness
by Georgia L. Jones

Samantha Garrett lives and dies a good life in the human world. She awakens a new creature, Samoda, a vampire-like warrior in the army of Nuem. She is forced to realize that she has become a part of a world that humans believe to be only "Legends of Darkness." Samoda finds her new life is entwined with the age old story of greed, love, betrayal, and vengeance.
[Urban Fantasy, ages 14+]

The Legend of Gwerinatha
Branwen's Garden

by Brad Parnell

Young Robert journeys to another world. There he comes of age amid a feuding government, grotesque monsters, an ancient ancestor ...and a couple of teenaged girls. With the help of a young wolf named Louie, Robert is introduced to the wonders and perils of a strange land called Gwerinatha.

THE ORDER OF THE WHITE GUARD
LITO'S CHILDREN: BOOK ONE

by Bryan and Wendy Schardein

In the year 1223, the Catholic Church establishes the Order of the White Guard to contend with unique foes that are a far cry from those of the Knights Templar: vampires. The members of the order are exceptional themselves. They're garou – werewolves.
[Epic Religious Fantasy, ages 14+]

VINE
an urban legend

by Michael Williams

Amateur theatre director Stephen Thorne plots a sensational production of a Greek tragedy in order to ruffle feathers. But as he unleashes the play, he draws the attention of ancient and powerful forces.
[Redneck Greek tragedy, 14+]

AN UNFORGIVING LAND RELOADED

by Jason Walters

This collection of horrific short stories from Nevada's Black Rock Desert will give you nightmares for years to come. The very landscape of the desert it portrays seems to have a will of its own, as if possessed by a violent, hideous determination to purge all visitors from its bosom. It suffers only those few who need nothing.
[Horror Short Stories, ages 18+]